TELEPATHY

TELEPATHY

A NOVEL

Amir Tag Elsir

Translated by William Maynard Hutchins

مؤسسة قطر
Qatar Foundation

دار بلومزبري - مؤسسة قطر للنشر
BLOOMSBURY
QATAR FOUNDATION
PUBLISHING

Bloomsbury Qatar Foundation Publishing
P O Box 5825
Doha, Qatar

www.bqfp.com.qa

BLOOMSBURY and the Diana logo are trademarks of
Bloomsbury Publishing Plc

First published in Arabic in 2015 as *Taqs* by
Bloomsbury Qatar Foundation Publishing

Copyright © Amir Tag Elsir, 2015

Translation © William Maynard Hutchins, 2015

British Library Cataloguing-in-Publication Data
A catalogue record for this book is available from the British Library.

ISBN: PB: 978-9-9271-0189-2
       eBook: 978-9-9271-1806-7

2 4 6 8 10 9 7 5 3 1

Typeset by Newgen Knowledge Works (P) Ltd., Chennai, India
Printed and bound in Great Britain by CPI
Group (UK) Ltd, Croydon CR0 4YY

To find out more about our authors and books visit www.bqfp.com.qa.
Here you will find extracts, author interviews, details of forthcoming
events and the option to sign up for our newsletters.

AUTHOR'S NOTE

O NE DAY A WOMAN whose mouth spoke one language and whose eyes spoke many, asked, "What's your view of the sun?"

I replied, "It's what I want beaming down on me."

"And the moon?"

"It's what is never eclipsed, even when it is eclipsed."

"The sea?"

"It's what will never be merely blue."

"Love?"

"What I can sense but never see."

"Man?"

"Someone striving to be a man."

"So how do you write?"

"By sun, moon, sea, love, and man."

A.T.

WHEN I WROTE MY latest novel, *Hunger's Hopes*, in only about a month, driven by its many inspirations and multiple twists and turns, which suddenly and effortlessly revealed themselves to me, I never imagined it would bedevil me with an apparently intractable problem, that I would be pursued by the nightmare of its associations, or that despite all my efforts, I wouldn't be able to escape.

I had returned from a splendid trip to Kuala Lumpur, an Eastern city that had stirred me profoundly and that I hoped to write about one day to capture its mischievous vigor. There I met cultural luminaries, capitalists, teachers, women of the night, and bums in the street. A number of personalities I encountered intrigued me, and in their distinctive appeal I recognized prototypes for characters in a novel, ones that would enrich any novel. Liyung Tuli, or Master Tuli as they called him, was one of these potential characters who dazzled me. He was an extremely well-known acupuncturist, and I noted his fitness despite his age, his very sincere smile, his extreme elegance, and the way he shed light on an ancient Chinese profession. The secretary at his clinic, Anania Faruq, whose nationality

I did not know for sure – a common occurrence within the mix of ethnicities in that tumultuous city – was also a memorable character. Her unusual height, her heavy use of cosmetics such as green and red eye shadow, her dresses that did not defer to any known style, her shoes fashioned from canvas and reinforced cardboard, and the army of patients and their companions who flirted with her overtly or silently, made her a living model for an Eastern princess who undertook an impetuous journey to a repressed Arab land – in a novel that had to be written someday.

I also met the erstwhile American academic Victor Grayland, who had become Hoshi Hisoka, a professor of music in a Japanese institute. He was a truly amazing guitarist, who, as he put it, performed for children and their mothers anytime, anywhere. He had left his native country in 1977, never to return. We became acquainted in a narrow corridor in the Chinese market which was packed with merchandise, people, and trinkets. In a number of subsequent meetings, we debated the question of his identity at length – how someone who had been born in America and had lived there till he was forty could become an honest-to-goodness Asian bearing an ancient Japanese name that meant warrior.

This academic was an old man but vigorous and so slender that he seemed a specter. His presence in Malaysia was part of his regular routine; he visited every year because he loved it madly and because he was a patron of Tuli's acupuncture clinic. As he himself said, he had never suffered from any ailment that required placing needles in his head, hands, or legs and hoped to reach one hundred standing on his own two feet. Acupuncture was merely an annual prophylactic for him. He always returned to his adopted homeland better equipped to deal with life after this treatment. His philosophy about erasing his Western identity and acquiring a different, Eastern one was simply that when you love, respect, and offer the East valuable services, it will never forget you. It weeps for you fondly when you pass; you will find some old man beside whom you sat in a public garden or a compartment of a high-speed train walking with his head bowed in your funeral procession, and the eleven-year-old daughter of your neighbors will place flowers on your grave at every propitious occasion. It was precisely the opposite in his native country, where geniuses, discoverers, and space pioneers died daily – as a result of traffic accidents, brain clots, and sniper fire in the streets – without anyone missing them.

To my way of thinking, his theory was dotty and based on weak arguments, but I didn't debate it much. I knew the man was a Leftist who opposed capitalism and what he termed America's foolhardy policies. He considered the country's numerous wars – especially the Vietnam War and more recently the invasions of Afghanistan and Iraq – to be major offenses that even the greatest historical eraser could never wipe away.

Strange stories cluster around Bukit Bintang Street in the center of Kuala Lumpur. Referred to by Arabs themselves as the Arabs' Street, it harbors Eastern and Western restaurants, giant shopping malls, and massage parlors, which can turn at any moment into dens of vipers. The beggars tint their bodies every color of the rainbow. Tourists stagger under the sensory assault: displays of Canon, Nikon, and Yashica cameras, accordion and saxophone players, and shredding guitarists who stage rowdy music parties at street corners, traffic lights, and all the people who cluster together or go about their business.

I was fascinated by the numerous coffeehouses. I hoped to become addicted to one of these (or have one addict me to it) so I would come to it daily to write – the way I do in my country – but that didn't happen, sadly, because I was so busy throughout the trip.

Everything inspired me and motivated me to write.

I returned home delighted with all these memories, feeling my blood pumping, my juices flowing, and expecting a new novel to steal over me at any moment. During my ordinary, daily life, when I lacked inspiration, I would be fortified by these memories; I actually prepared myself to be ravished by this new novel.

I thought that Master Tuli, the practitioner of Chinese acupuncture, would probably become a practitioner of passion's fire in the chest of a vanquished lover or that the heroine would have fallen in love but been conquered, against her will, by another. She might be the secretary Anania Faruq, that savage princess who sauntered down savage lanes, searching for a man she had seen for a moment in a primitive museum and had never forgotten. Hoshi Hisoka, the Leftist, would be a professor of political science

4

at a university overflowing with students and the instigator of a giant revolution that would blow through my writings and bring a mighty dictator to power.

I considered transferring all the commotion of the streets and public gardens to my country, which is stagnant even though it suffers from numerous hardships. Effendi Irfan, the taxi driver who was my companion throughout my stay there, would definitely make an appearance. He immersed me in details of his past and present life and shared his desire, long postponed, to perform the duty of the Hajj pilgrimage. He would be a driver here too but of a different vehicle – one that was grimy and pathetic, a marked contrast to the type of richly appointed vehicle he had driven all his life.

But none of this happened, and there's no hope it will now that I'm embroiled in the entanglements of *Hunger's Hopes*. I certainly never thought it would turn out to be such a dangerous novel when, with unconscious exultation, I wrote it.

THREE MONTHS BEFORE I traveled to Malaysia I published *Hunger's Hopes* with a local publishing house. A medium-sized novel consisting of 220 pages, it discussed in a purely imaginary way, which bore no relationship to reality whatsoever, a man in his forties named Nishan Hamza Nishan. Illiterate most of his life, Nishan worked as a messenger in an elementary school, where his job was to prepare tea and coffee, to fetch the teachers' breakfast, and to race between the different offices with a folder, documents, or requests. With unusual perseverance he had taught himself to read and write and had obtained his elementary, middle school, and secondary certificates, completing the last of them not long after he turned forty-five. Shortly before he was to enter university, after deciding to study law and become a judge, he contracted seasonal schizophrenia, which ran in his family and which afflicted him for a month or two every year. He would hear imaginary voices calling him. He would experience internal conflicts and pick fights with people, with life. He made ragdolls, stuffed them with explosives, and tossed them at elegant men and pretty girls in the streets. He might carry a sharp knife and attack random people with it. He might also wear a mask portraying a public figure such as the country's president or chief justice, or even a famed fruit seller or tailor, and then act as if he were that person. When the symptoms of schizophrenia disappeared or gradually diminished, he would return to his ordinary life, remembering only what people recounted and apologizing to everyone who had suffered during his frenzies. He would resume his perpetual efforts to study law.

Toward the end of the book, on a normal day without any delirium, Nishan experienced a strange weakness. He felt that his intestines were contracting, that his body was burning hot, that his head was spinning, and that his chest had become a battleground where pains struggled for supremacy. He staggered, without anyone's assistance, to the government hospital. There he was methodically examined, and it was discovered that he had incurable glandular cancer.

The novel was filled with many characters, including a high-society lady who always put on airs; a miserable soldier who attempted to overthrow the government without knowing how and who was executed by a firing squad; a truck driver who was a member of Nishan's family and who was charged with supervising him during his episodes of delirium; and a nurse named Yaqutah, whom Nishan met and fell in love with when she worked in the psychiatric hospital. She tried to help him during his ordeal. Nishan Hamza, however, was the puppeteer who held the strings for all the other characters.

Actually, in almost all the works I have written, I have devised strange names for my characters, names that are

7

not frequently used in this country, or names that are used disparagingly and in certain tribes. This has not been true for all my characters, of course, but just for those who play major roles or those I want to stick in the minds of readers. I never use three-part names; I don't know why I used the tripartite name Nishan Hamza Nishan in this novel. I noticed this fact during my feverish writing, but its rhythm prevented me from deleting it. I sensed then that I wouldn't like it if it consisted of only two names.

I knew no one named Nishan and have never encountered anyone with that name in my readings or frequent travels around the country or abroad. I mused over it when I first wrote it, surprised and wondering where it had come from, but have never reached a definite answer. Doubtless it was a known name and was certainly used in some Arab or African countries – just not in mine.

I remember the book's launch party was held just two days before I traveled, in a simple hall normally used for wedding parties. The event drew readers and people interested in culture. A beautiful girl asked me in a captivating voice with attractive circumspection: "Sir, how do you select names when you write? I find that the name Nishan Hamza Nishan is a perfect fit for the hero's character and behavior. If he were a real man, this would be his name."

I didn't have a logical answer for her question and had no coherent theory about names or precise strategy for choosing them. I couldn't even claim decisively that the names I wrote actually resembled their characters in the texts. All the same, I liked the attractive girl's question and was flattered that she felt I had cloaked my hero in an appropriate name.

I replied, "It's just something I sense, my dear. Nothing more, nothing less."

It seemed that another character – Nashshar, a perfume vendor in the old market who was wall-eyed and who also appeared in a number of twisting alleys in the novel – was admired by another girl in the audience, because she stood up at the event with a beaming face and asked, "Will I happen to meet Nashshar in the old market one day? If so, will he flirt with me?"

I said, "Perhaps."

She smiled and the rest of the audience did too.

Among those who attended the book launch and lined up to get their book signed was a man of about forty-seven. He was slim and his back was slightly stooped. He wore traditional garb: a thobe, turban, and shoes made of cheap goat skin. His stance seemed a bit shaky, and he kept turning around.

He was the sort of person who would attract attention at any gathering and actually had attracted mine, despite the crowd, the many questions asked, and the haste of some people to obtain a "sound bite", as is often the case at cultural affairs. I saw him rub against a young girl in the queue ahead of him – in a manner that seemed unintentional and caused by his agitation. The girl, who was wearing makeup and eye shadow that did not coordinate, turned toward him, frowned, left the line, and headed out carrying a copy without a signature. I saw him open the

9

book, peruse it for a moment, and then close it. When the man finally stood before me and placed his copy on the table for me to sign, he didn't hold out his hand to greet me the way the others had. He dropped the copy carelessly on the table and stood there with a distant gaze that swiveled in whatever direction his eyes chanced to look, without focusing on anything. I asked him his name so I could write a dedication for him in the book. He turned toward me, providing me an opportunity to notice in his eyes a gleam that quickly passed.

He said, "It's not for me. I'm going to give it to my sweetheart, Ranim. I'll bring you my own copy to sign some other day. Just write: To my precious sweetheart, Ranim, with my love."

I wrote the dedication to his precious sweetheart, Ranim, with his love, not mine, on the first page, and held the book out to him. He grasped it quickly and proceeded to stagger off. He was certainly an odd fellow, just as agitated as could be. I had never met a man of his age with such an obvious tremor, wearing traditional clothing, who was supposedly a passionate lover of a girl named Ranim. Ranim is a name used only recently here and it would be impossible for a woman of his generation to be called that. But I didn't brood about this much and soon totally forgot him in the throng of people who clustered around me – among them close friends who wanted us to conclude the evening elsewhere.

When we eventually went out to the street after the event, Ranim's shaky lover was still staggering around the area, carrying *Hunger's Hopes* in his right hand and a lit cigarette in his left.

Suddenly he approached me with quick steps and then stopped in front of me. Panting, he asked me without any introduction, "When will you return from your trip, sir?"

His question would have been perfectly normal if my trip had been announced. But I wasn't attending a cultural conference (so no one would have heard about it that way), I wasn't seeking medical treatment so that a journalist might have written that I was ill and traveling abroad for treatment, and I didn't remember referring to a forthcoming trip on my Facebook page.

It was a personal trip, one of a series I take from time to time to see a new country and to acquire the bits of information I need desperately for my work as a writer. I hadn't even told the friends who were standing with me then and attempting to shield me from a man they thought was an assailant.

I said, "I don't know" and moved away as I tried to think of the source from which Ranim's lover (as I thought of him) might have learned about my travels. I couldn't come up with any leads, however. To spare myself further anxiety, I tried to convince myself that this man had merely guessed I was planning to travel – nothing more. Even so, I didn't sleep well the two nights prior to my departure. I would wake up with a groan in reaction to the acid reflux I experience every time I feel agitated or stressed out on account of the book I am writing. In a grim dream I saw Ranim as a tender girl in the embrace of a beast; her lover, who bore no resemblance to storybook lovers, hit her with a signed copy of *Hunger's Hopes* and disfigured her with a lit cigarette in his left hand.

As I headed to the terminal carrying my suitcase, I sighed deeply and attempted to imagine a new country from which I might return with extraordinary Eastern spices that would get prose boiling on the hearth of my writing again.

– 3 –

T HE FIRST THING I did when I returned from my
splendid Malaysian trip was to seek out Umm Salama.
She is a middle-aged widow whose military husband died
in the Southern War while it was raging a number of years
ago. She has two adolescent children bursting with curiosity, but her limited means curb their enthusiasm. She lives
in a district far from my own and comes two or three times
a week to clean my house and prepare my food.

I live in an excellent district in the center of the capital,
in a house I purchased long ago. I am not married and have
absolutely no intention of marrying again after my divorce –
from a woman who loved me and whom I loved – seven
years earlier. My ex-wife simply could not bear to live with
the lunacy of my writing and perpetual travel, my bouts of
pessimism and frustration, and the troupes of women who
are always twittering at cultural events.

My house actually has been very well fortified against
surprise visits of any type, and just a few people know
where it is. By and large, no one visits me except my only
brother, Muzaffar, who works as an aid coordinator for an
NGO and who lives in a city in a distant region in the
west of the country. He only comes twice a year, not to

spend time with me but to hang out with his friends in the capital, which we residents normally find less thrilling than do people who live in the provinces. On a few occasions, Malikat al-Dar visits me. She is an elderly, retired midwife and my spiritual mother, as I call her. She was a friend of my mother's and helped me a lot when I was starting out. I normally meet my friends and readers, however, in numerous coffeehouses. This strict domestic isolation has permitted me to organize my library the way I want. I have put most of my books in the living room and created two smaller libraries in the two adjoining rooms. Meanwhile, the master bedroom has remained free of everything related to reading and writing. When I enter it, I bring along only my drowsiness or my insomnia – nothing more.

Although I resigned from my post as a middle school math teacher a long time ago and haven't practiced any other occupation since, I have managed to eke out a living, one way or another. It's true that the furnishings of my house are very modest, but I respect that and love their modesty. I do not possess the latest car like those that brokers and social parasites drive, but my cranky old car, a Toyota Corolla, performs its duties on most days admirably and satisfies my limited transportation needs.

The next morning, entranced by the Eastern writing spices I had brought back, I was busily attempting to drag them onto paper when my cell phone rang. The call was from Najma – a presumptuous girl whom I had known for two years and whose arrogance still made me grumble occasionally. She felt so superior to the world that she seemed even to breathe sparingly. She felt superior to the nation and its inhabitants and was fully convinced that the distant stars in the sky had been named for her — not the other way round.

Najma dressed traditionally and didn't follow modern styles, because she didn't care to be swayed by the fashions of this age or any other. Her perfumes were a mix of local and foreign scents so she wouldn't feel confined to one fragrance, as she explained. Her opinion of men could be summarized in just one sentence, and it wasn't favorable.

I met her one day at an out-of-the-way coffeehouse where she read me her story "The Neighbor's Goat". The idea was imaginative and remarkable. One of the writer's neighbors owned a kid that could forecast the weather, volatility in prices, illness, and death. When the goat raged violently through the house, its owner knew that a military coup, a destructive earthquake, or some similar catastrophe would occur that day. Although the story showed a fertile imagination, it was poorly written.

I told the girl frankly what I thought and that she should rewrite it after she read more authors and acquired more literary skill. She did not like that at all. She quarreled with me and broke off contact with me for a number of months. She returned again, however, when she found herself in a quandary that she wanted to implicate me in — not to resolve it, because she would be able to resolve it on her own, at the appropriate time, as she put it — but for me to transform it into a novel.

During that period, she had moved with her family to an old district that was inhabited in the main by people with limited incomes, because her father had retired from a government post in the tax bureau and his resources had shrunk considerably. There, a young man who drafted legal documents in front of the Shari'a Court and who lived in that district, saw her and fell madly in love with her.

At first the young petition writer, named Hamid Abbas but known in the neighborhood as Hamid Tulumba (or "the Pump"), displayed his affection merely in swift, breathless looks at her face and trim body whenever he chanced upon her in the street. This display of affection evolved into the release of ill-phrased exclamations, when he found her waiting for a bus or taxi at the district's public transport station, and finally became thick letters with long, convoluted sentences. She would find these along the district's dusty roads, at the publicity and advertising agency where she worked, or tossed over the garden wall of her house. Sometimes one of her little brothers would bring a letter to her when he returned from playing in the street.

Laughing, Najma informed me with her extraordinary arrogance that she loved this situation immensely and wanted it to simmer for as long as possible so that it could serve as a splendid literary plot in the future. She had devised for the poor petition drafter all types of mud for him to sink in up to his hair. She had plied him with colorful smiles, carefully traced on her lips. She had provided him with glimpses of facial features that could easily be described as those of a dazzling, agreeable girl. Once, she dropped a white piece of paper in front of him with only a question mark on it. One day she wore a screaming red dress and misted her body with a powerful jasmine perfume, because Tulumba had once written she was a red rose that emitted its scent incessantly.

Her dilemma, when I encountered her that day, had apparently reached a climax, and her lover, Tulumba, had informed her in the last of twenty letters that had reached her by various means, that he was preparing a house of love to embrace both of them, building a ceiling over it with a trellis of affection, and furnishing it with soft pillows of love that would never fray.

"Ah! Isn't this a splendid novel, Master? Isn't it a plot concept worth putting into words?"

In fact, it was by no means a splendid plot idea for a novel that contemporary writing would embrace. Stories of unrequited love, of requited love, or even of love between one hundred different partners have become so shopworn in all the literatures of the world that I believe they no longer attract mature readers. Moreover, even though I didn't know that unfortunate petition writer and never expected to meet him, I sympathized intensely with him and hoped that he really wouldn't need to pull his heart out of the muck and that his true-life ordeal would end. Besides, even if I had found the story concept convincing, I wouldn't write it, quite simply because I don't write from experiences that don't involve me at all. I have never written a novel based on an experience that some random person had and that I happened to hear about. I have my own loose-fitting storytelling shirt that never feels too tight on the body of my writing. I have my imagination, my taste, my perfumes, my spices, and my paved and rocky roads that I traverse when I ride forth on writing's back.

That day I didn't laugh, even though I wanted to laugh till I died. I asked the sadistic, supercilious girl, trying not to anger her, "Why don't you write it? Aren't you a writer?"

She replied calmly as her right hand tapped her chest gently, "Of course I could write it, but it wouldn't enjoy a large circulation, and that's destined to happen when an established author publishes it. I want you to write it and delegate to me the task of enjoying reading and promoting it."

"No . . . " I said without thinking, as if the computer on which I write my manuscripts had spoken. "No . . . no, I don't write stories like this."

That day, when Najma assumed a variety of colorings — primarily anger, indignation, and nervous tension — it seemed to me that she might actually be really captivating and attract many crazed admirers in addition to Tulumba, if her heart were to become more like those of ordinary people and if feelings were inserted into her — not lofty ones — just ordinary emotions.

I watched her hands. Their movements reminded me of a defeated person still struggling valiantly for victory. I observed her eyes a little and discovered that they lacked the limpidity of normal eyes. They seemed to be fitted with contact lenses to shield dark secrets that shouldn't have light shed on them. She didn't move from her place but adjusted her posture. She struggled till the hint of a smile found her mouth.

She said with a suavity I did not expect, "You will write it for my sake. Isn't that so? Every writer offers gifts to girls who are his fans. This will be my gift from you."

I remembered that she had read me her story "The Neighbors' Goat" in a corner she had chosen in a noisy coffeehouse that I did not frequent often and that none of my friends patronized. She had paid for my coffee and my cigarettes that day, had listened to my negative opinion of her story, and had left angry, only to return with a dilemma that was hers and not mine.

In my first meeting with her I had probed a lot into her character, more than I should have, but had found no trace of admiration that would prompt me to offer her a text that I could not write. I was certain now that she, even if she had never read a book by me, would understand from my approach to writing that if I did actually write her dilemma as a novel, I wouldn't elevate her a single centimeter. I would make her the worst heroine ever. Her "lover," on the other hand, the petition writer Tulumba, I might transform into a crazed lover who would not accept defeat easily. He would bring her to dwell in a house trellised overhead with vipers and furnished with daggers and knives. He would kill her time and again so that he could survive as a firebrand of love, eternally aflame.

Annoyed with her and her insistence on creating a victim, I sided strongly with her suitor just as I had sided previously with numerous individuals I considered victims of an unjust life. I remember that in my novel *The Course of Events* on the final two pages I saved the hero – Sufyan, an embezzling bank employee – from serving many years in prison because I considered him a victim of a lengthy chain of malfeasance, in which he was merely a minor link, while much more robust links were watching his tragedy and laughing.

In the novel *Tortoise*, published five years ago, I watched Salma, a cruel, perverted public security officer who devised innovative forms of sexual torture, die on the last page; but then I invented an effective remedy that extended her life long enough to give her time to apologize repeatedly to her victims before she expired.

I said to Najma, "My dear, I don't owe anyone anything. I'm a free writer and write only what I want and what I can. The experiences of other people don't appeal to me or excite me."

I think I was rude, because I felt wasted and had a bitter taste in my throat. I saw the supercilious girl vanquished this time so decisively that she made no attempt to inch toward victory.

She plucked her classic gray handbag from the table, opened it forcefully, and took out a strip of aspirins. She popped two pills from the strip and swallowed them without water. Then she rose and turned away from me.

She departed with quick steps, much faster than a girl's ordinary gait. The adolescent waiter, whose smile revealed teeth corroded by sweets, had, I suspect, a different scenario – involving love and the flight of the beloved – playing in his mind at that moment. When I returned to my house that day, I sat brooding deeply about the petition writer Hamid Abbas, reflecting on his nickname Tulumba – "the Pump" – and how he had acquired it. This chain of thought was far removed from Najma's dilemma and was a line of reasoning that might introduce this crazed lover to a different text far removed from his actual life.

Najma did not meet with me again for a long time after that – just as she hadn't after I criticized "The Neighbors' Goat". So I was surprised to receive, approximately a year later, on Facebook, a request to be her friend. I responded quickly and did not resist my desire to check out her wall to learn what types of projects she was working on, whether she was still writing short stories, and whether her skills had improved.

I found the story "The Neighbors' Goat" plastered across the page, with all its linguistic and technical flaws. There were hundreds of comments and expressions of admiration surrounding it, promoting its flaws.

I discovered another story by her, called "Espionage Report on My Grandmother". The idea was excellent, but the writing wasn't. The best thing about the story was its title. There were also other brief phrases that did not match her personality, like: "My heart burgeoned in your flank. Straying in your feelings, it rises, soaring ... I beg you," or "If my desire to meet you dies, don't forget to visit its grave."

I placed a "like" sign on a picture of her in dark clothing and without accessories, leaning against a mud-brick wall, apparently in some village or country estate, even though I didn't actually like the picture. This "like" opened a passageway in the wall of our quarrel and we met once again.

When we met, I intended to ask her about Tulumba, the wretched petition writer – whether he still was madly in love with her and was creating scenes for her immortal novel. But I didn't, for fear of becoming involved in her crisis again. She, for her part, gave me no information about what had happened. She also did not refer on her page to that dilemma, which she had said she was trying her hardest to drag out as long as possible.

I answered Najma's phone call after a number of insistent rings.

She spoke in a very low voice, as if she were too good for the line and did not want to release her voice full force. She apologized for not attending the book launch for *Hunger's Hopes*, citing an unexpected illness of her normally healthy grandmother, who was over ninety, and enthusiastically invited me to attend an enlightening debate to be held the next evening at the Social Harmony Club, where she would introduce the speaker. The lecture would be devoted to something called "reflexology medicine", about which there was currently a lot of talk. "People have a right to understand its reality from the experts, in person, and the degree to which it can alleviate pains and treat chronic illnesses," she said.

Despite my serious efforts to acquire information and despite the fact that I have expended endless hours reading books of every type, all I knew about reflexology was the name, and it had never occurred to me to learn about it firsthand. The topic had never interested me much, and I had no wish to seek treatment, should I get sick, from any alternative form of medicine. The invitation was delivered persistently, however, by a girl who had been humiliated by me often; I had to go, to humor her.

– 4 –

I WAS A LITTLE LATE arriving at the Social Harmony
Club – which was near my house – because when
I had already dressed to go out and was ready to leave, I
was suddenly overwhelmed by some literary passages that
I considered extremely important. I wrote down the title
of a possible novel, part of the plot idea, and some random
scenes that might make it into the final text or that might
be torn up straightaway. I was inspired to think that this
novel might include some characters from Kuala Lumpur
such as Master Tuli and Anania Faruq and some other local
characters that I wouldn't need to research, since I had them
squirreled away in my memory. I wished I hadn't become
ensnared in this invitation from Najma so I could continue
writing all night long, because I had a strange feeling that
the writing would flow and not peter out until I became
exhausted.

It was after seven-thirty when I found a parking spot
near the venue, parked, and entered the hall. Luckily the
lecture hadn't started yet.

The place wasn't as crowded as I had expected it to
be. I noticed a number of individuals I knew, sitting in
front, their eyes focused on the dais. Among these was the

elderly trade-unionist Abd al-Rahman, who used to head the main labor union. He had called himself "Mahatma", even though he did not go barefoot, wear a loincloth of cheap fabric, or harangue people in the streets — as he should have done to earn that title. Since he used to complain of chronic back pain, he was no doubt searching for relief through reflexology. I also noticed Sonia al-Zuwainy, who owned a successful chain of hair salons. She was of Moroccan origin and had been married and divorced many times. She must have been searching in reflexology for a way to moderate her temperament so she could stick with one man. I noticed the swim coach Shawqi, who was called Shushu by his swimmers. A fourteen-year-old boy sat alone on an isolated chair with his eyes glued on the stage; I didn't understand why, unless he was hoping the lecture would provide a laudable way to attract girls.

I plopped down in the first empty chair I found. This was next to a middle-aged woman wearing heavy gold earrings and an attractive, green thobe embroidered with gold thread. I hoped that my presence would not be noticed by anyone I knew or by any of my readers and that the evening would pass uneventfully and I could continue writing afterwards without any burdens or encumbrances. The woman, however, noticed my presence, although fortunately she did not have a clue who I was. She leaned slightly toward me and asked in a whisper, "I think I've seen you before. Do you give the weather report on TV?"

Without hesitation, I replied, "Yes, occasionally."

I glanced at the stage, where Najma was sitting. She wore an ordinary white outfit like a nurse's uniform. The speaker, who was beside her, was elegant in a black striped suit and a yellow necktie. Behind them was a large poster on which was written in broad, blue letters: "Reflexology Medicine: Pros and Cons: A Lecture by Dr Sabir Hazaz."

Najma introduced her guest, using the title "professor", which wasn't by any means an outstanding title in a country that addresses in this way office boys, vagrants who sniff gasoline, guys who sell newspapers on the street, and electricity meter readers. I used to know a parking concierge at one of the big hotels who bore this title. The credentials that earned him this sobriquet included his ability, no matter how many cars there were, to find a parking place for a driver. I have a cousin who is a carpenter in a small shop and who two years ago produced by himself all the doors and windows for a merchant's house of several stories. Then he awarded himself the title of professor; he wouldn't saw a wooden plank or tighten a screw on a wardrobe that was coming apart unless the client addressed him by this title. Even Steven Riek, the Southerner who sits in a wheelchair in front of the old Church of the Virgin in the center of the city and draws amateur pastel portraits he sells to passers-by for two pounds is known as Professor Steven Riek. The Ethiopian woman Dama'ir, who used to work as a maid for one of my acquaintances and who occasionally came up with totally novel recipes, was called Professor Dama'ir. At a panel where I spoke on the state of youth writing, I was accorded the title professor but immediately scrapped the

26

idea and explained that I was just an ordinary novelist and possessed none of the qualifications for a title like this.

Najma plunged into the lecturer's biography and enumerated his various forms of expertise, all his successes, and the numerous trips. He had treated an Arab leader for savage migraine headaches that the Americans with all their facilities had been unable to cure. He had treated Africans who were dogged in their countries by psychological complexes and cured Communists who still believed in Lenin and Marx of their ingrained beliefs. He had practiced this profession for the love of God in countries that could not offer him even a loaf of bread and in areas that electricity still hadn't reached, whereas his theories of reflexology were studied in the most advanced institutes in the world.

The man was very short and very thin, but his fingers were as long and graceful as a pianist's. Although his face was relatively free of wrinkles, he was definitely over seventy.

The lecturer launched into his speech right away in a large voice that belied his small stature. "Reflexology is a concept that relies on exciting certain points on the hands and feet by massaging them in a special way. This provides an excellent treatment for many health problems. It is not a new science, even though people have not heard much about it till now. Most probably its origins date back more than 5,000 years when the Chinese knew about it and used it to remedy health problems. Ancient Egyptian drawings of it have been found, proving that they knew about it as well. Each of their kings had reflexology physicians who supervised his care. For this treatment to provide the hoped-for results, the body has been divided into ten vertical regions, with five on each side of the body, starting from an imaginary line bisecting the body vertically. Treatment must be provided by a specialist's hand; it cannot be something haphazard performed by a person without the requisite skill.

"But what happens when the regions we have referred to are massaged?

"There are actually numerous theories about this, but most probably reflexology treatment influences the body's blood flow, just as massage assists relaxation, and thereby helps the body perform its functions in a better way. By this method, we undertake treatment of numerous diseases like anxiety, insomnia, puerperal fever, irritable bowel syndrome, chronic back pain, the menstrual problems of some women, sterility, frigidity, premature ejaculation, even various types of cancer, inflammation of the liver, joints, and prostate, and . . ."

I suddenly felt bored and envied Professor Hazaz his effusive vigor and blazing mind. He would pause occasionally, breathe deeply, wet his throat with a sip of water from the full glass in front of him, or cast a brief glance at a folded piece of paper that a member of the audience had certainly submitted to inquire about some ailment or to request some clarification.

I needed to move a little, to smoke a cigarette, or to flee from the place to return to my draft. I didn't feel at all absorbed in this lecture. I was not enjoying it and had never thought I needed reflexology treatment. To date,

I have had a limited number of pains that I have loved and lived on friendly terms with for a long time: nervous tension while writing, bloating of the colon, acid reflux, insomnia on some occasions, mood swings – but nothing else. If I required treatment in the future, Sabir Hazaz would certainly not be the person I sought out. I decided to rise from my seat while the professor was enumerating the dangers of treatment conducted by a non-specialist. These included torn tendons, an increased need to urinate, and thickened discharge of the body's morphine, leading to something akin to insanity. Najma looked bored too. Her expression was reserved and her eyes almost closed. Her diaphanous white headscarf had slipped, but she had not lifted a hand to adjust it.

Even though the audience was small, people had begun to slip away without embarrassment. A young woman whose name I don't remember, although I see her occasionally at cultural events, was taking notes on a piece of paper as if she were a pupil in an important lesson.

It seemed to me that Mahatma Abd al-Rahman wanted the professor to stretch him out right then and massage the map of his feet, because he was holding them out in front of him and kept pressing them together. The seat of Sonia al-Zuwainy, the hair stylist, was empty, and the isolated youth remained alone. The swimming coach, Shushu, was shaking his long hair rapturously, and my middle-aged neighbor, the woman with the embroidered green dress and heavy gold earrings, leaned toward me again the moment I started to rise. She whispered, "Now I

recognize you. You courted me when we were in secondary school. You've matured a lot, but I know you with a
woman's memory. How are you, dear? Are you married?"

I didn't reply and quickly shot outside.

I stood in a rather dark corner of the outer hall of the
club building, smoking my cigarette deliberately while I
tensely revisited my Asian memories, hoping they would
speak again quickly so I could record them the moment I
returned home.

The hall, unlike the inside chamber where the lecture
was held, was very crowded. At a number of tables people
of different ages were eagerly playing dominoes and cards.
People were speaking shrilly about the current political
situation, the faltering national economy, and local football matches. A few people were gathered around an old
table-football board situated in the opposite corner, waiting impatiently for their turn.

It was a run-of-the-mill hall in an ordinary club where
the presence of a novelist, even a stellar one, would definitely
not attract anyone's attention. The people there were far
removed from the paths of reading. All the same, something
unusual happened at that moment. I suddenly saw Ranim's
troubled lover emerge from an inner room. He was wearing his same traditional garb – thobe, turban, and goatskin
shoes – and heading rapidly toward me. In his right hand
was a copy of *Hunger's Hopes* and in the left was what in my
alarm I imagined to be a lethal dagger.

I quickly tossed my cigarette on the floor and hurried
toward the exit, fighting a painful urge to scream and

summon the people busy playing to protect me as if I were attacked by a lunatic. Scenes and memories raced through my mind: what I had and hadn't produced during my lifetime, what had been really happy and what painful. I thought about the curse that writing is and told myself that it is the greatest curse that could afflict a math teacher who otherwise might today have become Minister of Education or at least a noteworthy educational adviser.

For the most part, my writing has been a mix of reality and imagination – something inspired by my surroundings and something I invent. But even when I find inspiration from reality, I don't write it down the way it is but rather change it so that it won't wound anyone; I don't allow reality the chance to assert its dominion. Friends, family members, neighbors, acquaintances, activists and recluses in the world have found their way into my writing, yet no one has ever said, "That character's me." No protagonist of a scene I borrowed has ever repeated that this was his scene and that he would kill me for writing about him. I don't even use the real names of cities for fear a city will come forward one day to claim I have depicted it. Even though I have described in many passages the liveliness of my street, not one of its residents has ever reproached me.

When the man stood before me, to my intense astonishment, I flashed through all of *Hunger's Hopes* and called to mind all its characters, cul-de-sacs, alleys, paved streets, and rocky paths. I pondered its inspired and uninspired parts, what I considered brilliant in it and what I thought was flavorless and vile. I finished my review without finding anything that resembled this man or that would cause him to pursue me this way.

The novel was in his right hand; what I had imagined to be a lethal dagger was a figment of my imagination, because his left hand was empty.

Shaken, I tried to relax, fearing that he would run away from me. I asked the man, "What do you want from me? Why are you pursuing me?"

He smiled or perhaps laughed — I couldn't tell which. All I could discern was that his wide mouth opened some-what and his teeth confronted me, although tobacco had marred them so much that none of them could really be called a tooth. I thought I heard a sound that might have been the clearing of a throat prior to a laugh.

He said, "I brought my copy of *Hunger's Hopes* so you could sign it for me. I told you before you traveled that I would bring it to you one day. Do you remember me? Do you remember the copy you signed for my sweetheart, Ranim?"

"Yes, your sweetheart Ranim; who could forget some-thing like that?"

I didn't ask him how he knew that I had returned from my trip and had been conned into attending this lecture. It seemed to me he was stalking me or could predict my movements — I didn't know for certain which.

I took the copy he was holding out to me as my shaken resolve to flee grew. I searched my pocket for a pen but didn't find one. Then I saw the man dig into the pocket of his thobe and pull out an old blue pen without a cap.

"Take this," he said in a harsh tone, offering me the pen.

"Your name, sir, so I can write the dedication. You didn't mention it last time."

With calm, deadly firmness, he replied, "Nishan Hamza Nishan."

"Who?"

I suspect that I was quite agitated. No, I was only upset momentarily. I pulled myself together as best I could. Here was a crazy man who was trying to provoke me, but I wasn't going to fall for his provocation.

No one has a rare name like this, at least not in the combination I had struggled hard to concoct to avoid any possible repercussions. No one is named Nishan Hamza Nishan except the lunatic who dwells inside the pages of *Hunger's Hopes* and whose fate I sealed, feeling no remorse and leaving him no further options, when I gave him glandular cancer and wrote that there was no hope for a cure. Had the man said his name was Muhammad Hamza or Hamza Ahmad or any familiar name in common circulation in the world, I would have believed him. If he had said Nishan Abd al-Mutallib, for example, or Abd al-Ghani Nishan, I would also have believed him. Even if he had said he was Nishan George or Mark Nishan, I might have believed him. But for him to claim the full three-part name, just as it appeared in my text, was totally incredible.

I grasped the book with uncharacteristic braggadocio, which I feign occasionally in fleeting moments of weakness in the hope that the person challenging me will feel he is confronting a mountain. I opened the book to the first page

33

and wrote, with the pen the man had loaned me, "To Dear Nishan Hamza Nishan, in memory of a profound and stirring encounter during a chance meeting. With my love."

Then I signed my name the way I always do, wrote the date and place clearly, and handed the book and pen back to the man. I searched for my cigarettes to smoke a new one to make up for the one I had tossed away when he appeared. But the story, unfortunately, did not end here. Instead, it became even more unsettling. This surprising novel was about to have a new beginning – one I had never anticipated or included in my calculations.

Ranim's shaky lover, aka Nishan Hamza Nishan, as he called himself, accepted the signed copy and his old pen but then, unexpectedly, pulled his identity card which was dated more than six years earlier, from his pocket. He held it before my eyes, which were wide open, long enough for me to read all the seals and signatures and even to see the grease spot on one edge, not to mention the web of tiny cracks on the side of the photo, in which he wore an open, dark green shirt. With thick black hair and a carefully trimmed beard, he looked a more appropriate suitor for a woman named Ranim and therefore more like the Nishan Hamza Nishan I had written about.

I was obliged now to accept my moment of weakness and to respect the snare that neither the man standing before me nor I had endeavored to construct.

I had used his full name in one of my novels. That was certain. I had not known that anyone in the world possessed this precise name. Just two minutes earlier I had felt contempt for him when I wrote his name on the dedication page. A deep-seated certainty had been prancing around inside me then that I had encountered the rare reader who had not been content merely to read a book but had borrowed the hero's name as his own. I had previously wondered how my hero's name had come to me. Now, after this surprise, I suspected that I would never reach a conclusion.

I knew a little about theories of telepathy and extra-sensory perception — how a person tens of thousands of kilometers away might be able to transmit a message to you. A man in an extreme crisis might send out an SOS and the woman he loved might rush to his rescue. A soldier in a ruinous war caught in an ambush or an oppressed prisoner striving to terminate his persecution, and so forth, might also send out a telepathic SOS.

Why, though, would Nishan Hamza Nishan send me his name telepathically and how could I have received this name when I claim no gift for receiving telepathic messages — unless perhaps I have this talent but hadn't discovered it yet? Besides, were such theories actually true or were they just speculations that lacked powerful supporting arguments, although they had infiltrated people's minds?

I have mentioned writing *Hunger's Hopes* faster than any previous novel, driven by powerful inspiration, as one road block after another vanished. I had not suffered from any writer's block worth mentioning, and the events had seemed to form an organic chain that created its own links. In an isolated corner of the lobby of a mid-range hotel, where I felt at home and where I have written most of my books, a splendid Ethiopian waitress named Hasanat kept bringing me black coffee, the way I drink it; but she was forced to remind me frequently that my coffee had gone cold, because I hadn't even noticed the cup on my table or the charming Ethiopian waitress who brought it. Given all this, perhaps I should not have been surprised to discover now that Ranim's lover dictated the novel to me, without my realizing it.

Hunger's Hopes definitely contained many lackluster passages together with flashes of inspiration, powerful scenes and weaker ones, fates that were harsh and unfair, and others that were totally predictable. What I hoped for most now was that its plot would differ from this man's life story.

"What do you say now?" he asked. His hands had begun to tremble, and his voice acquired a tremolo as he spoke.

"I need more clarification, please," I replied, or tried to reply. I'm not actually sure, because my voice sounded quite distant.

"I'll tell you everything," he offered. His face looked clouded – I could see him but not clearly. The cigarette in his hand had burned down to a stub, but he still grasped it.

The lecture on reflexology ended then, and Najma came out of the lecture hall looking as if she had just been liberated from a long, boring period of incarceration. Professor Hazaz, who was beside her, seemed even livelier than before. He was walking elatedly, handing out his business cards to everyone – even to the people who were busy playing dominoes or who were talking excitedly about racquetball matches.

Najma approached us and greeted me vivaciously, touching me on the left shoulder. She extended her right hand languidly to Nishan Hamza, who told me in a brief aside that he would wait for me outside. The professor greeted me quickly and then departed. Najma chatted for several minutes, but I didn't retain much of her chatter. As she left, she asked me to comment on what she was going to write on her Facebook page: "Your comment is important, Master."

I didn't feel she was captivating just then and felt no desire to read her post about a lecture that had quickly bored me. All I wanted was to find the solution to the puzzle that had suddenly popped up before me. If this suggestion of telepathy had surfaced while I was writing *Hunger's Hopes*, I definitely wouldn't have published a novel by this name.

5

I<small>T WAS A LITTLE</small> past ten p.m., and I was extremely tense as I drove my jalopy through the virtually empty streets of the capital, not knowing where I was going.

The car radio was tuned to the national broadcasting station, and a politician from the ruling party was talking about the great revolution awaiting the nation after gold was discovered in numerous regions and the great economic progress, encompassing all citizens, that would soon occur. I scarcely heard him. Nishan Hamza sat silently next to me, staring at the road without focusing on it. He returned from time to time to the same folded page of *Hunger's Hopes*. He would read a little and then close the book.

He had felt it necessary to speak to me, and I needed that conversation even more than he did. He wanted to share a secret with me. I wished his secret could be broadcast now on the radio instead of forming part of a conversation studded with useless small talk.

I couldn't sit with him in some coffeehouse, whether one I frequented or one I didn't, because by this rather late hour all the coffeehouses had closed. I couldn't go with him to my house, because I was afraid of taking a lunatic there – and that's what I thought he was. He might become enraged and kill me in a frenzied moment, and I would die pointlessly. Even if he weren't a lunatic and didn't harm me, I didn't want anyone to know how to find my house, which I mentioned I have fortified carefully to protect my seclusion. I couldn't just drive around like this expecting him to talk, because I don't absorb things when I'm driving. Besides, I was perturbed and definitely needed a place where we could sit and talk while trying to relax so I could calm down.

The shameless politician concluded his radio interview. Now they were broadcasting "The Migratory Bird" by the genius Mohammed Wardi, and I sensed the song's brilliance for the first time.

Observing that my companion had suddenly put his hand in his pocket to search for something, I was alarmed. An acid reflux attack ensued and my breathing almost stopped. His hand finally emerged, however, grasping the old pen without a cap, and he wrote some type of note at the bottom of the page with the folded corner.

Two weeks before my trip, my brother Muzaffar had visited me, although as I have mentioned his visits don't involve me much, because he doesn't spend a lot of time with me. He would not return for six months, but now I wished he would show up so I could forcibly enlist him in my predicament. I would oblige him to shield me or at least volunteer some sensible opinion. Naturally I could have informed one of my close friends – I actually thought about that. I scratched this notion, though, at least until I fully understood what sort of crisis I faced, because perhaps there was really no crisis whatsoever. It might have been one of those pranks we encounter from time to time. I might have endured something much worse than this before but couldn't remember now.

I was surprised when Nishan spoke. His eyes weren't directed toward me, and his voice was odd. It was the quavering voice of a feverish man. "Where are we going, sir? I think you've been driving for more than an hour and seem to have no intention of stopping."

I had no ready answer for his question. I really had been driving without any destination or any interest in finding one. I looked around to get my bearings and was astonished to find myself in the Railroad District, near the central train station. This was where my spiritual mother, Malikat al–Dar, lived. Actually I was almost in front of her house. I had no idea how I got there. Some invisible rope seemed to have dragged me. All the same, I felt a certain degree of relief, because my spiritual mother's house was my second home, which I visited whenever I wanted a mother figure, the scent of a mother, or food prepared by a mother. It wouldn't seem odd for me to arrive now with a guest, because I had done that frequently, most recently two months earlier when I brought a former storyteller named Isma'il. I had wanted some information about the capital's ancient history. He had refused to provide these clarifications until after a repast of traditional home cooking. Malikat al–Dar's house had been virtually the only place where I could find an old-fashioned meal.

Malikat al-Dar's house was expansive, not physically spacious but emotionally so. Thus at any time it might shelter strangers or people from her village in the North of the country – villagers who were clueless in the capital. The room she allowed me to use was at one side of the relatively large courtyard. It was a rather big room that was furnished with cots and quilts and a small cooler containing water and occasionally food.

The house's main entrance, which was directly opposite me, had been repainted a dark green; the sign announcing that the occupant had performed the Mecca pilgrimage had also been repainted: "Pilgrimage Accepted, Sins Forgiven, and Praiseworthy Return." Malikat al-Dar had fulfilled this religious duty once with her husband and another time after he died as a member of an official delegation. Her income from her evening job, which she still retained – as a nurse for a well-known gynecologist and obstetrician – even after she retired from working for the government, was enough to animate her household and her whole life.

I knocked gently on the door, and she opened it herself. She was limping a little. She had symptoms of osteoarthritis in her knees because of her plumpness and advancing age, and these symptoms had become more severe. An orthopedic physician had told her she would need knee replacement surgery soon.

It was late and the house seemed empty. The beds in the open guest room appeared to be unoccupied, and the quilts were folded up. The sound of a colicky infant echoed from one of the inner rooms. I deduced that he was the child of her daughter Fatima, who had been quite pregnant during my last visit (before my trip to Malaysia).

I asked, "Has Fatima given birth?"

"Yes. Her son, Dhu al-Nun, was born nine days ago. You weren't here for me to tell you. When did you get back?"

I wasn't at all surprised that this newborn had been given a name that far outstripped his age and that was unlike the names of other contemporary newborns. I knew that Malikat al-Dar and her family loved strong names and imposed them on their in-laws, even if they were foreigners. They regarded modern, wimpy men's names through eyes filled with pity and regret. Malikat al-Dar had three daughters, each of whom had married and given birth to boys with names like Abd al-Basit, Abd al-Qayyum, al-Tanajiri, Abu al-Ma'ali, and Suhayb.

I didn't have a chance to see Fatima, who was resting with the nuisance named Dhu al-Nun, because of the calamity accompanying me: Nishan Hamza Nishan.

I thought Malikat al-Dar hadn't noticed my companion in the faint light of the courtyard. But I was wrong, because as we crossed the darkest area of the courtyard, she asked, "You haven't introduced me to your guest?"

I would introduce her to my guest, since she was welcoming him into her home; this was an unavoidable evil. But I wouldn't pronounce his full name or even part of it. I would limit myself to his father's name, Hamza, which was a common enough name. I didn't think he would object. My problem was that she too had read *Hunger's Hopes*, although without understanding everything – like other

42

old-fashioned midwives whose educations were limited. She had read it not because she loved reading or was fond of culture in general, but simply because I had written it. She would certainly know that Nishan Hamza Nishan was the lunatic who dwelt in that novel. If I pronounced his full name, I would raise dozens of question marks for which there was absolutely no need.

I said, "My friend Hamza. He's a writer who has recently begun to make a name for himself. We were driving around, talking, and suddenly found ourselves near your house."

She didn't say anything and brought us into a room she normally used to receive transient guests, as opposed to the clueless ones who stayed for extended periods with her. It was an excellent room that was thoughtfully furnished with a large settee and chairs covered in red velvet, as well as two beds made of polished wood on which any tired guest could stretch out. She left us and then returned a few minutes later carrying two glasses of orange juice with ice. She departed, explaining that Dhu al-Nun needed her expertise in the care of newborns in order to quiet down. I knew that she had detected a hint of mystery and wanted to distance herself from it.

Nishan's telephone and mine rang at the same time. His ringtone was rather strange and sounded like distant barking. My ringtone is very common – it's a cheerful song that I swear is on three-quarters of the cell phones in this country. I didn't answer my phone; it was a call from Najma, who no doubt would ask me to comment on something she had written on Facebook about her seminar with Hazaz. I turned off my phone, but Nishan quickly answered his. Although I wasn't certain, I thought he was speaking to a lady. The voice was shrill and gushing; I could hear some from where I sat. He responded with the word 'yes' more than ten times. Then he shut off his phone and turned toward me.

Now, as I listened to his story, I would understand what I had done to him when I wrote *Hunger's Hopes* and what he would do to me. He reached for the glass of orange juice, brought it close to his mouth, but set it down again without taking a sip. He cleared his throat, and then began to speak. I became a pair of large ears, something that hadn't happened to me for a long time.

6

I T WAS ABOUT ONE in the morning when I dropped Nishan Hamza Nishan off in the Wadi al-Hikma District, a neighborhood being developed on the western edge of the capital. Although it may well become an upscale neighborhood in the future, in its current condition it resembles the miserable district I described in great detail in *Hunger's Hopes*. I had never visited it before, because I have no family or friends who live there.

Nishan Hamza was calm except for a slight tremor of his hands and feet, and appeared to be extraordinarily alert mentally. He clasped his copy of *Hunger's Hopes* firmly in his right hand while he groped in his pocket with his left hand for a cigarette, although I suspected that he had run out of them. I handed him what was left of my pack and told him as he stepped out of the car that I would return to meet with him again. I didn't give him my telephone number or ask for his, for fear of consequences I didn't feel like incurring then.

Most of the houses in Wadi al-Hikma were unfin-ished skeletons of concrete and red brick. Some were one story, others had two, and a few stretched even higher. In front of them were cots with frames of rough

45

wood and webbing woven from torn ropes. Men hired as sentries to guard the houses were stretched out on these. Other homes, constructed from canvas, corrugated metal, and tree trunks, were scattered through the area. These appeared to house poor people or migrants from remote areas, fleeing war or famine. They had built these shacks on vacant lands that hadn't been developed yet, and the inhabitants would doubtless be forced to evacuate them when the true owners of the property returned and began building. My companion's home was one of these huts.

Electricity wasn't readily available there, and thus the depressing, faint light of scattered gas lanterns provided the night with desolate depth. I thought no one here could have read *Hunger's Hopes*. Where there was no intellectual vigor, there would certainly be no reading. As long as Nishan said nothing about this calamity, no one here would know anything.

Before leaving, I made several quick turns through the district in my car pursued by dozens of barking dogs. Then a number of the recumbent sentries rose from their cots to investigate the situation.

I wasn't alarmed but didn't really feel calm either. I experienced a moment of extreme neutrality that I'll attempt to maintain for as long as possible while I search for suitable answers to the striking eeriness I experienced for more than two hours while I listened to Nishan Hamza in the home of Malikat al-Dar. I was trying hard to comprehend all of this but not succeeding.

Nishan Hamza Nishan in the novel *Hunger's Hopes* was the same as the real Nishan Hamza Nishan. His family had emigrated from N'Djamena in Chad during the rule of the dictator François Tombalbaye at the start of the 1960s. His father had settled in the Sudanese capital, where he had worked as a guard for a private residential development. He had made special efforts to find his son work as a messenger in an elementary school when Nishan was ten, and his son had continued working in this position till he was thirty, when, at the prodding of the young pupils, he embraced education. He began to study and finished all his school exams through to the secondary level in two years. Then he worked hard to enter university and study law, only to be blindsided by the symptoms of seasonal schizophrenia. That had obviously impeded his progress.

During his first bout of illness, Nishan had fallen in love with a nurse named Yaqutah who actually served as a nurse in the government psychiatric hospital until last year. She had done her best to care for him during his ordeal. But she had suddenly disappeared, changed her name to Ranim, and traveled to work in Libya once it was liberated from Gaddafi's rule, after she found a position there.

The aristocratic lady, who vaunted her superiority, without or without cause, was Su'ad Mu'tasim, the owner of the building where Nishan's father worked as a security guard until he passed. She had died as a result of a blood clot in the brain last year. The ambitious soldier, who had attempted to overthrow the government without even the attributes that would have qualified him to lead a fringe football team and who was executed after the attempted coup along with his comrades, was a dead ringer for Asil Muqado, a member of Nishan's tribe, and had embarked on the same adventure. He came close to seizing power but wasn't executed, because he fled at a decisive, climactic moment. Now he was living in his ancestral homeland, Chad, where he bragged about being an adventurer who had almost succeeded.

Nishan's life story was very close to events in *Hunger's Hopes* – even the page where I had suspended any grounding in reality. That was the folded page Nishan kept reading and annotating at the bottom when he sat beside me in the car. It was page 120, when the hero again succumbs to seasonal schizophrenia.

Some of the names were real – Nishan, of course, and the nurse Yaqutah, although the end of her story was different. In the text she retained her name to the end, cared for the hero till his last moments, and wept for him when he passed. In real life, she changed her name to Ranim and traveled abroad in search of a better life. Asil, similarly, fled instead of being executed. In my novel, Su'ad Mu'tasim did not die of a blood clot; she died halfway through my work of liver failure. The work on the whole, however, consisted of true-to-life pages that described the life of a poor, desperate, marginalized man, who had communicated his story to me in some fashion and had even made me fiddle with the details of some passages, while I retained his name, life story, and present circumstances. Because the text was actually published, while reality was stuck at the folded page, neither Nishan nor I could say definitively whether his end and the novel's would converge.

But how had all this happened?

"How has this happened?" I asked him with icy limbs, a pounding heart, and a mind that was totally blank.

He didn't know, and no one else could know, I believed. Something strange had happened. I had simply to accept that it had happened and strive to find some explanation for it if I could. I had to forget I had once visited Kuala Lumpur with its mischievous vigor and returned with Eastern spices that were going to produce a novel. I was obliged to work to create for this man a better destiny than the one I granted him in the text. Success in this effort would not be entirely in my hands or within my powers, but I had to attempt it. I felt a warm sympathy for the man and thought of a number of steps to take. I asked him, "Did you know about me before *Hunger's Hopes*? Had you read any of my other works?"

"Because of my circumstances, I don't read literature or anything else on a regular basis. I'm a poor man whose education came late in life — but I definitely knew about you. I had read some isolated chapters from your novels in the newspapers. I also read some of your interviews and essays, which I didn't understand too well."

"And *Hunger's Hopes*? How did you happen to read it, since you don't read many books?"

"Someone I know who lives in the district brought me a copy when he found my name and story in it. He was enraged when he handed me the book, because he thought

49

I knew you personally and had narrated my story to you to write."

"Was he one of the characters who appear in the novel?" I asked, gripped by anxious fear that I might have written about some ordinary person and distorted his life enough that he would wish to destroy me, especially since he got hold of a copy of the novel and actually read it, only to discover his neighbor and his neighbor's story inside it. What I found most unusual was that Nishan was acting normally and hadn't attacked me or accused me of anything.

"No, he's not in the novel," Nishan replied as he silenced his old cell phone, which had begun to ring persistently.

I sighed with relief. I was spared that then.

Another question: "The Chadian man who purchased your sister Mabruka when she was a child and disappeared with her to unknown reaches of Africa – was he real? And your sister, herself – do you have a sister named Mabruka?"

"No, I don't have a sister or a brother. I was an only child. Now I'm the only one left, as you know."

Questions began to multiply in my mind and raced toward my tongue. What about the truck driver who bound Nishan with ropes when he was delirious? Or the perfume dealer Nashshar, who loaned him money from time to time? How about the exploding dolls – did he actually throw them at elegant men and beautiful girls in the streets? Did he take his treatment seriously? Did he go to prison, as happened in a passage in the novel, for example? But these questions were quashed when Nishan suddenly changed. I saw his eyes redden, his lips quiver, his hands gesture convulsively in the air, and something like thick slobber drool from his mouth. He cried out in response to an imaginary voice calling him: "Wait for me, Rabi! Wait for me, I beg you!" I thought he might shatter one of the glasses of orange juice over my head or smash one of the velvet chairs. He might escape into the interior rooms and strangle Malikat al-Dar, Dhu al-Nun, and his mother, Fatima.

I couldn't predict what a lunatic might do in his delirium, because I had observed people like him in moments of sudden frenzy. I'll never forget a youth I saw one day in my neighborhood – he had throttled his male organ with a circular piece of rusty metal, and it exploded in front of me.

I stood up quickly, feeling alarmed and guilty for paying attention to him in the first place and then for bringing him inside a household that respected and honored me. I grabbed his hand and dragged him out of the house as best I could. I was panting, because he was heavy and rigid. I pushed him into the car's back seat and searched wildly for a rope to bind his hands and feet. Despite her age and cranky knees, Malikat al-Dar came running out with Fatima's husband, her son-in-law. They asked what the problem was and I insisted that there was no problem, that my friend the writer had simply had an epileptic fit, and that I was rushing to find medical assistance for him. Nishan had calmed down a little, luckily, and I was able to drive him to his house without any fear.

When I finally reached my house after three a.m., the street was still busy, in a city that never quiets down.

The trappings of a wedding that apparently had taken place on the street in front of a nearby house were visible; drowsy workmen were trying to guard the temporary pavilion and chairs but not faring too well, because I saw a couple of men in ragged clothing put several chairs on a donkey cart and flee with their booty.

I spotted a trembling shadow in front of my house. Thinking that it was Nishan Hamza, I felt alarmed and drove around the block a number of times. When I returned, no one was there. I realized I would never fall asleep and would pass the remaining hours before the morning's commotion as a wakeful fool, waiting impatiently for the arrival of all the bustle so I could slip into it, pursuing any openings it might provide me with.

I sat at my desk in the living room, which was crammed with books, and turned on the computer. I cast a quick glance at the Kuala Lumpur file, and it seemed to me that what I had written thus far was merely contemptible scribbling on the wall of a novel that was destined to go unwritten – during a period when no novels would be written.

The Chinese acupuncturist Tuli was there, and the features that made him so striking had begun to be sketched: his lavish elegance, his carefully crafted smile and the way he bowed repeatedly before every visitor and rubbed his fingers from one moment to the next. But I felt in no mood for him – not at all. For the American-Japanese Leftist Hoshika I had chosen a perilous future in a country that he did not comprehend. He would never live to be a hundred here, although that was what he aspired to. I had sketched the secretary Anania Faruq, outlining her eyes with antinomy, decorating her hands with dark henna patterns, and dressing her in an embroidered Sudanese thobe. I had reached the stage of planting her in potting soil so that she would grow to be captivating but fully capable of inflicting harm. I was in no mood for her now and felt opposed to any attempt to revive her. I wouldn't proceed any further with her in the text.

There was a Chinese alcoholic named Yanyan, who had a room near mine in the Kuala Lumpur hotel where I stayed. He would knock on the door of my room every night for no apparent reason. I had made him an entrepreneur visiting a country that lacked the wherewithal for drunkenness. I depicted him undergoing the distressing complications of alcohol withdrawal. Now I would leave him dangling as well.

I closed the folder of my thoughts and entered the world of Facebook in an attempt to forget what was happening around me. I stumbled upon Najma's traces. She had switched out her personal photo for one that showed her without a headscarf and with her hair permed. She had written a number of lines about her event with Professor Hazaz. As usual there were hundreds of likes and comments. Some of her friends criticized her for not inviting them to the event. I added my "like" and wrote: "What a splendid evening!" I quickly clicked on another page which seemed like a treasure to me, of a girl calling herself Nariman. That might actually be her name or perhaps it was a fantasy *nom de web* for a world that was both open and frequently conservative. On her page she had assembled friends who could never have assembled in real life. Among those friends were bearded and turbaned men who had fallen head over heels for the temptation she represented. They referred to her as "Virtuous Sister" and competed with each other to describe qualities of which they were ignorant and to write what they referred to as chaste love poetry about the eyes in the picture posted showing a girl wearing a niqab that revealed only her eyes. She wrote verses, discussions, and aphorisms and advocated virtue as well. Her friends included enigmas like Bird Milk Vendor, the Anti-Christ, Mobile Charger, Tartura Sorceress of the Happy Home, Wounding Breeze, and I'm the Chameleon. Many wrote silly remarks, discussed their frustrations, or were content to add a swift "like".

I read a new poem by someone calling himself Sheikh Ma'ruf. It celebrated the large eyes on a face that was radiant even when covered. There was a pressing call from a person – Love-Struck Rural Guy – for her to remove the veil from her picture and simply wear a headscarf to show her piety or to send him an altered photo in a personal email because he had a surprise for her. Since a clear picture of a Kerry Cleaning Machine was at the center of the page for no apparent reason, someone had written: "We need that to clean our hearts."

I smiled and left this unfamiliar atmosphere. I returned to my own page and wrote: "Telepathy." I didn't expect any comments. I closed the page on that strange world, filled with everything a novelist needs.

Suddenly I remembered the folded page in *Hunger's Hopes* – page 120 – and began to rummage through my shelves for the novel, now that the state of neutrality that had seized hold of me after midnight had lifted. I was sure I still had a number of copies somewhere but couldn't think where I had put them. I searched my living room, where most of my books were shelved, with mounting anxiety. Then I moved to the two rooms I use as branch libraries. I discovered all the works I have written, even those I have dropped from my vita and never mention in statements or interviews. I didn't find my most recent novel, although I had to have at least one copy of it. Perhaps I had given all the copies to my friends. Perhaps I had put them some place I couldn't remember. Perhaps I was daydreaming and had never written a novel called *Hunger's Hopes*. I finished my search of the house, looking even in my bedroom where only my slumber or insomnia intrude, although I was certain it wouldn't be there. I went outside to search the car, where I triumphantly found two copies in the boot.

I lit a cigarette and impatiently opened the book to Nishan's page. I began to read noncommittally, like any neutral person without a vested interest in the topic. I wanted to check where Nishan actually was, even though I could almost recall the entire novel and could replay it in my mind, as I had at the Social Harmony Club. He himself had told me where to find him in the novel.

I read:

For the second year in a row, something happened to Nishan Hamza during August, which was hot and humid despite an occasional, autumnal cloudburst, to shake his stability and ambition. It was after Nishan filed his application for admission to the national university, just when it seemed that he would be admitted and that his ambition to study law and become a judge would be realized. Many of his acquaintances and neighbors in that neglected district had mocked his desire, asking, "Why law school, Nishan?"

He had replied with a laugh, "In order to prosecute Sahla the hairdresser for oiling women's hair."

In the district, people were organizing a number of voluntary campaigns at the same time. One set out to spruce up the district at the behest of residents who knew nothing about sprucing up besides the words. A campaign against disturbing the public order was led by Mas'ud the Nurse, who was without doubt the greatest threat to public order in the district. They entrusted to Nishan the leadership of a third, exceptional campaign against envy.

But who was there to envy in this impoverished place? What was there to envy among people who were alike even with regard to constipation and diarrhea and to the way they were ground between the jaws of misery and hunger?

"Just lead it, Nishan."

He led the campaign but discovered — as the low, mud-brick houses or the dwellings made of random scraps of corrugated metal did too — that everyone in the district was envious and envied. One man envied another his tunic, which was washed and starched, while someone else envied the first man his shorts, which didn't have a single rip or patch. One fellow envied a beggar his mellifluous voice that attracted almsgivers, but the beggar envied him his full head of hair. One woman envied her neighbor for being able to light a cook-fire that day, and the neighbor envied her for having a son who was taking enlistment exams and might become a soldier.

Nishan was engrossed in this campaign, which he directed without excitement or passion. Together with members of his team, he strove to sift people's souls thoroughly to remove envious feelings from his district's residents forever.

No one would ever envy anyone else there again. If the existence of such a feeling proved inevitable, it should be one-sided — all the residents might be envied by strangers who didn't and wouldn't live in the district.

During the past year Nishan had experienced some unusual symptoms that simple people attributed to jinn they said were breeding inside him. Some people who healed with amulets attempted to evict this tribe of jinn but failed. When he became truly dangerous and started making ragdolls packed with explosives and lobbing them at pedestrians in the capital's congested streets, he was arrested and ended up tied to a worn-out bed in a psychiatric hospital, where he was treated with injections of tranquilizers and electric shock therapy. There he fell in love with a nurse named Yaqutah, who came from a background comparable to his. Her tribe had African roots like his. This nurse lavished care on him, told him about herself, and allowed him to say whatever he wanted to her without interruption. Nishan seemed to make a full recovery and after his release strove to maintain contact with the woman who had befriended him during his delirium and fever. He visited her at the hospital, watched for her on the roads she traversed, and rode public buses with her, conversing with her all the way. She frequently loaned him money that he was unable to refuse.

Now that he was able to love freely, he was considering marriage, the way a normal person would, conducting himself in his neighborhood circumspectly, and spearheading the campaign against envy. Eventually his symptoms returned, though, and he became agitated, suffered from nightmares, heard voices calling him, and searched for means to hurt other people to ensure that he himself would be hurt. At moments when he was thinking clearly, he wept alone in a tumble-down, corrugated metal house, on the streets, or in any dusty nook he found to rest.

The page with the folded corner ended with a clear convergence between real and fictitious elements. I interpreted it the way any reader would: as an SOS tossed into my life's waters, muddying them.

Night had ended and the morning's raw materials were in evidence: the sounds of vendors selling bread and milk door-to-door, of school pupils, of car horns, and of strident jackhammers. I retreated to my bedroom, to which I brought insomnia and grief, and tried to avoid thinking – but failed.

7

A T EIGHT A.M. SHARP, not feeling sleepy in the slightest, I installed myself at the home of my old friend Abd al-Qawi Jum'a, who was commonly known as "the Shadow". He lived in an excellent house, constructed of bricks painted a gleaming gray, in an upscale district called Al-Zahra, near the airport.

Abd al-Qawi the Shadow, who was eighty-nine, was an actor, lyricist, and playwright. He hadn't aged, and the fountain of his creativity had never stopped gushing. He became famous for stirring songs he composed in critical periods of the nation's history and for his satirical and lach-rymose plays. His drama *Straw Blood*, which he produced in the mid-1980s at the National Youth Theatre, where it ran for an entire year, was a masterpiece that people have never forgotten. Nine years ago he dramatized my third novel, *Well Secret*, under that same name. At the time it enjoyed an excellent reception.

I needed to consult the Shadow and draw on the experience of a master and the wisdom of a sheikh regarding the topic that had robbed me of sleep; I knew it would keep me awake nights and prevent me from reading or writing till I resolved it.

I broached the topic of Nishan Hamza Nishan, the man I had unconsciously written up in *Hunger's Hopes*, with the Shadow directly, without lengthy preambles. I was obliged to drink his bitter coffee and to share his breakfast, which consisted of two boiled eggs, with no salt or spices. I also had to drink a glass of sour orange juice that I knew for certain would give me indigestion and create acid reflux in my esophagus. I was also forced to participate in his exercises that were designed to strengthen his core abdominals and that he ran through without showing any sign of fatigue or panting while he was stretched out beside me. He thumped me roughly on my belly every time I slacked off because I was tired.

Once we finally finished his obligatory morning routine, as he referred to it, and he allowed me to breathe normally and light a cigarette, the Shadow seemed intrigued by the case. He asked me to repeat my tale in fluent literary language as if it were one of my novels. I didn't understand why he requested this and couldn't comply, because for me writing a novel is a type of insanity I cannot perform in the presence of an observer, not even that of a creative genius like the Shadow. In any case, though, I repeated the story.

"You know," he observed, "this tale reminds me of my old play "An Elderly Demon in the Republican Palace," which landed me in prison at the end of the 1950s. Writer, do you remember that play?"

Actually I didn't remember it and had never before heard it mentioned as one of his plays or by another author. This was quite simply because I had not been born then and did not remember it being published in book form.

Without thinking and without sensing that a trap had been set for me, I said to humor an old man's youthful memory, "Yes . . . yes. I remember it most definitely."

As his eyes sparkled gleefully, he said in a sharp but not offensive tone, "You certainly do remember it because you laughed when you watched it in your mother's belly. You clapped loudly at the end of the performance."

I felt a bit embarrassed and wanted to apologize by explaining my conduct as having been caused by preoccupation with Nishan and by my eagerness to hear his take on this conundrum. The Shadow, however, did not allow me to do this. He waved his hand before my face, just as I was about to apologize, and continued, "It's not your fault . . . That great play, which was the first text the dictatorship brazenly criticized throughout the entire country, which shook people's confidence in their rulers, and which sparked a vanguard of street protests and even unrest in government circles, was one I absolutely did not write myself. Matthew, an Anglican priest, sent it to me in twenty-six consecutive dreams. I would awake each day and write down what had come to me in the dream without addition or deletion. Don't be surprised that Nishan has sent you his story and that he − not you − fiddled with some of its details. Do you understand now that this matter is ordinary, not astonishing?"

I suddenly felt that the Shadow had moved beyond the vigor of youth and graduated to the crustiness of old age.

I was about to express my opinion when to my surprise I sensed that even if he had just made up the tale, the circumstances were parallel. As I mentioned, I had never heard of that play and – now that I think of it – am sure I had never heard of Father Matthew either. I don't know whether a real person was imitating a real situation or whether this was a playwright's invention.

I asked, "What's the relationship between the stories of Matthew and of Nishan Hamza Nishan?"

I absolutely hadn't recorded dreams and had been conscious throughout my creative hysteria, observing my normal rituals – both admirable and vile – while I wrote *Hunger's Hopes*. I have noted that it flowed forth with no impediment worth mentioning. Perhaps that was the nature of the similarity between the dream Abd al-Qawi Jum'a could remember and the forgotten dream that insinuated itself into my mind while I was writing.

Abd al-Qawi the Shadow had risen from his recumbent position on the rope bed and stepped youthfully into a room that he used as an office and that overlooked the courtyard where we were sitting. As he left, he told me that an idea had struck him, even though it was before his scheduled writing time, which normally began at ten. He would just jot the idea down quickly and return. What astonished me about the Shadow was how entirely convinced he was that he was brilliant and world-renowned and the master of whatever situation he found himself in (or didn't). Consequently, he was treating me now, despite my age and fame, as if I were a novice who was wasting his time. I always remind myself when I meet with him that he is much older than I am and was a luminous star when I was merely a myopic toddler who could write nothing besides his own name. Though it's true that I haven't been influenced by him and haven't written drama or poetry while he hasn't written a novel, all the same I consider him my master and the master of my whole generation.

Half a minute later he returned shouting, "I found inches of dust in my office, and the sentence flew away. I'll remember it later when they clean the office . . . Linda! Ni'ma! . . . Dust makes thinking impossible."

He resumed his recumbent position on the rope cot. It was droopy, and some of the ropes had pulled loose. I was smoking, and my question may have been waiting at the tip of my tongue. Then it leapt out: "You didn't tell me how Matthew's and Nishan Hamza's stories are related. Did the priest sign his name? Did he know the characters, live with them, and then send them in the dream?"

"No . . . I really didn't expect this question from you, Writer. What is the relationship between a Christian cleric and a dictatorship? How could he play himself in a story criticizing the dictatorship? I said that he composed a play about the dictatorship in his mind and sent it to me so I could write it down on paper. He was in telepathic communication with me, without either of us realizing that, and this is exactly how Nishan Hamza communicated with you. The difference is that Father Matthew wasn't personally involved with the fate of the characters;

64

it made no difference to him whether the Republican Palace collapsed on the heads of the people working there. Nishan, however, came to you to change his destiny. You wrote in your novel that he dies of glandular cancer, and he doesn't want to die. He can live with schizophrenia and deal with it, since he won't die from it. But he's terrified of dying of cancer and is begging you to help him. Do you understand now?"

I understood some things, but other matters still escaped my comprehension. I told myself but not the Shadow this.

Why hadn't Father Matthew tried to record his play on paper himself, since he was the author? Why had Nishan tampered with details of his own story? Why hadn't he ended it with schizophrenia since he feared dying? There were no answers to these questions, which even lacked a framework of logic within which they could be answered.

Another question that I considered extremely important was now smoldering at the tip of my tongue: "How did you know it was Father Matthew who sent you that play telepathically rather than someone else? How did you establish that?"

Abd al-Qawi the Shadow laughed till his tight core abdominals quivered, and he raised himself from his recumbent position to sit upright on the bed. He was barefoot and his feet were slender but had some ugly scabs. He reached for the coffeemaker to pour each of us a cup, but found it empty.

He replied, "This is a secret I won't share with you. I haven't disclosed it to anyone. I promised Father Matthew fifty years ago I wouldn't tell anyone. Just two days ago I visited his grave and renewed my vow. What I want you to do is to show as much concern for your co-author as you possibly can. I took a special interest in the priest until he died. I actively supported him, because he added to my vita the important distinction of serving as a political prisoner."

I selected – from what I sensed would prove an endless chain – a final question: "Did you attempt to figure out how all that transpired? Did you arrive at a theory that explains his telepathic communication with you?"

"No . . ." the Shadow replied sharply. "I didn't feel I needed to."

A brown-complexioned girl with small breasts and short hair, which was massed on the crown of her head, appeared from inside the house. She was presumably either a maid or a family member. Carrying a feather duster, she headed to the room the Shadow used as an office. I had entered that room dozens of times. In my early days I had scouted what he was reading, having a look at the books lying around with pages turned down or folded. I occasionally borrowed a book that appealed to me, without asking permission, and then either returned it or not. Last year when we were sitting in his office, he handed me a short story written out by hand on glossy paper. He said it was by a young woman and asked me for my candid opinion of it.

I had taken the piece of paper and, glancing at it, discovered that it was supercilious Najma's story "The Neighbors' Goat". She must have brought it to him after she was angered by my negative opinion of it. I read it again carefully while he watched.

Then I observed, "Not fully cooked and lacks a lot of the requisite spices."

"Right," the Shadow responded as his old man's face glowed with a smile. "That's my opinion too. But that's not what I told the author. I'm not in the habit of expressing blunt opinions to women — not even when they write about manicures, shampoo, and Wella beauty products."

"So how do you avoid the potholes of their insistence on hearing your opinion? Do you flatter them?"

Abd al-Qawi the Shadow laughed, revealing teeth that were uniformly white and shiny. He must have a full set of dentures; no teeth, not even ones borrowed from jackals or hyenas, remain a bright, gleaming white and completely uniform on both jaws up to the age of eighty-nine. The memory may retain its contents and the body, with daily exercise, may stay fit, but teeth, which are crude grinding machines, cannot remain that solid.

The Shadow responded, "I manifest naughty senility toward them: the tongue's twaddle, my hands' gestures, and my eyes' lasciviousness. Then they leave me never to return."

I had laughed as I pictured that poor girl, who loved her story and came to present it to an expert, only to be confronted by an old man flirting in a way she would never have imagined. I could picture Najma in that situation and felt like laughing some more.

"What about male authors? How do you deal with them?"

"I vanquish them by chattering on about a past that I invent from whole cloth and about my frustration with writing. They don't knock on my door again after that."

The brown girl emerged from the room; the feather duster in her hand was all red now. She must have used it to remove the dust that had caused the adventitious sentence to fly out of the Shadow's head. He would enter his office now to begin his daily writing, which I knew would continue till three p.m. It was almost ten a.m., and I would not leave him time to feel anxious or to glance at his watch. I thanked him for his help, although he really hadn't helped me much. He hadn't told me anything that I had not already told myself in even greater detail when I considered Nishan's enigma: that this was an SOS from a fearful man who was awaiting a response from me.

As I headed toward the door, I asked, "Should I send you a copy of *Hunger's Hopes*? I've been preoccupied and haven't sent you your copy. I know you haven't read it yet."

"No need for that," he replied. "I borrowed my daughter Linda's copy after she read it. She'll certainly discuss it with you."

He lifted the pillow he had been leaning on, and a copy of the novel with its covers ripped off lay there. A sliver of wood that served as a bookmark poked from it. He did not ask me to sign it for his daughter, Linda. This was one of my great complaints about the Shadow — that he did not acknowledge the practice of signing books. He accepted unsigned copies of books and never signed published copies of his plays for anyone.

I traversed the streets of the Zahra District, driving slowly while I read the numerous signboards, which had multiplied in an astonishing way in the last few years. They advertised liposuction clinics, modern dental clinics that offered dentures with Hollywood-actress smiles, hair salons that listed services including blow-drying, perms, and coloring, tinsmiths, barbers, attorneys, legal accountants, and purveyors of conjugal happiness crèmes and pomades that grew lost hair. One clinic was devoted to the care of Akita dogs, bull terriers, and bulldogs. Another offered compressed oxygen technology for diabetics' injuries. It occurred to me that the entire country was selling something. I didn't know, though, who could be consuming all this — certainly not Nishan Hamza or the other inhabitants of his peripheral district, which had been settled by migrants, watchmen, and low-paid laborers. They would never buy a crème for conjugal happiness or a pomade to re-grow hair.

I found myself forced to think about Nishan again, after having forgotten him for some minutes. I brooded about ways that my secluded life would need to change and about how I was to handle adopting this lunatic.

Did I feel guilty for having "written" him?

I didn't know; it would have been unfair to expect me to feel guilty when I hadn't stolen anyone's particular characteristics. Something uncanny had organized it all and guided everything. I had released a novel that would neither enrich me nor add a new meteor or thrilling satellite to the universe.

Suddenly I caught sight of Professor Hazaz, the reflexology specialist whose lecture at the Social Harmony Club had so bored me that I had walked out only to be confronted by Nishan. Professor Hazaz, who was wearing a light green shirt and black trousers, climbed out of a late-model car – a red American Hummer – and glided swiftly into a white five-story building halfway down the main street. I looked up and down, taking in the whole building, and noticed a large sign on which was inscribed in elegant, sinuous letters: "Dr Sabir Hazaz, Specialist in Reflexology Medicine."

I smiled in spite of myself on seeing the skill of a simple masseur – like Musamih, who drove a Mitsubishi Rosa bus for the public transport authority and who was one of Malikat al-Dar's sons-in-law, and even by Umm Salama, who cooked and cleaned for me – practiced by this "Reflexologist" who drove an expensive Hummer, a brand that was virtually nonexistent in the country. On the other hand, an author who summoned and corralled ideas in his mind, where he reconfigured them before depositing them onto the pages of a difficult novel, might only too easily find himself entering prison or taking a one-way ride in a hearse.

I really did not envy Hazaz. The comparison between us was extraneous but inevitable for me at a moment when I was deciding whether I should continue to be a writer – plagued by the lunatic Nishan and other catastrophes – or return to my former career as a teacher of mathematics, the simplest principles of which I had forgotten and would be forced to review. I remembered that a man who used to manage an investment firm had once informed me that he loved my writing and wished to help me create a large and dependable income. All I had to do was shell out a small sum that I would watch grow before my very eyes; I wouldn't believe it once I was transformed from a mere writer with limited resources into a wealthy capitalist. I handed over to him whatever I could spare for five years and waited. It came as a grim surprise to me when the investment firm folded suddenly, its proprietor vanished, and I discovered that its former offices were an institute where some woman taught exotic dancing.

I noted the Reflexology Clinic's address in my agitated mind to remember it should I need to visit for some reason, and then quit the Zahra District and its environs.

My destination was exceedingly odd for a person like me. I was heading to the working-class Aisha Market, on the capital's eastern edge, to search for Joseph Ifranji, a Southerner who had separated from the South when it separated from the North, even though all the other members of his family had migrated to the new nation. He had worked as a messenger in the school where I once taught. Now he was worthily unemployed in the Aisha

71

Market, where he was attempting to enter commerce by any door he thought open, since he could not enter the world of middlemen through upscale revolving doors. I wanted Ifranji to be part of the changes I was introducing into my life. In fact, I wanted to hire him to handle my headache's ground zero by taking full charge of Nishan Hamza. I didn't think he would object. Indeed, this was an opportunity not to be sniffed at. Seen from Ifranji's perspective, the job would offer him a chance to relax, even if his companion would be a lunatic who had died in my novel and who in real life was threatened with death.

I had given up teaching more than twelve years earlier. Back then, Joseph Ifranji had been a slender-kneed boy who loved to run, to hunt plump birds, and to scale houses to collect trinkets. I had last seen him six weeks earlier when he had informed me that his wife, Ashul, had left, taking their son, whom he had named Mahogany in honor of a tree he had never seen. He had heard the name by chance while making his rounds in the market. His wife had deserted him for the new nation. Now his son was certainly eating clods of dirt in a fatherland that had yet to achieve its dream. It was hardly out of the question that the child would die of malaria, sleeping sickness, or any other of many ailments. I had cheered him up considerably that day by giving him five pounds. I had also informed him – even though I rarely tell anyone – that I had based a character partly on him in a work I had started years ago but had never finished. Now it was one of the texts I refer to as abandoned. Ifranji had seemed neither happy nor disappointed and had shown no curiosity about the character I based on him. Instead, he demanded ten more pounds and departed, wearing a soiled, wrinkled shirt and sandals that were torn in more than one place.

− 8 −

W E ENTERED WADI AL-HIKMA after more than an hour and a half of slow, awkward driving through anarchy and unbearable traffic jams. A truck driver who had "All Days Are One, My Love" painted on the back of his vehicle abused me with crazed persistence and cursed me vilely. Countless beggars weaved through the hubbub, heedless of the danger. Vendors hawked cheap pens, tissues, and dirty cloth bags insistently. The homeless boys who clog the capital's streets rubbed filthy rags on car windows and demanded payment for their services.

The day was fading away. In another hour, night would have set up camp with its pains and suspicions. Ifranji was on my right, rebellious and anxious but eager for this assignment that he didn't really understand, even though I had sketched it out for him. During the hours he spent with me in the Aisha Market and the Nu'man Real Estate Office, where I had rented a small, unpretentious house, and during the ride in my car, he had conjured up myriad characters. These included a bodyguard, an intensive care nurse, an alert watchman in an hour of danger. He would need to play all these roles while he looked after Nishan in order to allow me first to find him treatment for his schizophrenia and then to research how probable it was that he would eventually contract glandular cancer.

The tale of Nishan's telepathic communication with me and of his transmission of the novel no longer concerned me much — not at present anyway. I did not want to busy my mind with searching for its causes and how it had happened. Recalling it all yesterday had exhausted me.

What I wanted, quite seriously, was to counteract the arid destiny I had written and attempt to adorn it with some verdure, even if it proved obstinate and insisted on remaining dry. I wanted to perform what I considered my imperative duty, while stepping away from my career as a novelist whose works are distributed nationally and internationally, in order to be an ordinary person who would sweep his neighbor's courtyard if he found it dirty, milk a goat for an elderly woman with shaky hands, or carry a small child on his back while crossing a street bristling with traffic accidents. I thought this would not be out of character for me, because I have a benevolent personality and in the past repeatedly performed such chores. It was just that at this time, I needed to change my life's pattern to allow this character to succeed.

I first considered bringing Nishan to live in my house and placing beds for him and Joseph Ifranji in one of the library rooms. In that way I would be only steps away from the headache's epicenter. I changed my mind, however, when clear thinking supplanted my emotional reaction and I realized that the situation did not really warrant this. How could I know the consequences of having two strangers live with me, one of whom was insane and likely to die young – if my novel was accurate – while the other carried a troubled history on his back? I once wrote a novel about the ploys of desperate people whom I united in a single cohort by either putting them in prison or shutting them up in a room and allowing them to conspire together. I had distinct characters, who would never have met in real life, live for a month in a single house. The result was that the earth's gravest treacheries occurred in that house.

So I decided to rent a small retreat. That much had happened. What would happen next was for Nishan to move there and for Ifranji to abandon the rag he slept on in the Aisha Market and move in as well. If some crisis occurred, it wouldn't be in my house and wouldn't concern me. If Nishan rebelled against Ifranji, that rebellion wouldn't reach me and wouldn't affect me.

I developed my plans without consulting Nishan, because I felt sure that a person who begged for assistance telepathically would accept a volunteer's helping hand. Moreover, he hadn't merely sent the message, he had come once he was free of the symptoms of schizophrenia to greet me in person and narrate his life story in a balanced and orderly manner, right up to the moment he went into convulsions and appeared to be in serious danger.

At this stage the important question was whether Nishan would pose a threat to Ifranji.

Wasn't there some possibility he might kill him? In that event, I would regret not merely a novel I had written but blood I had played a part in shedding. I explained this possible threat to Ifranji forthrightly as he sat beside me while we were entering Wadi al-Hikma — after ordering him gruffly to take off the old, broken pair of sunglasses he was wearing, because I wanted to see and assess the reaction in his eyes.

He responded with a laugh, "No problem! The old Aisha Market, after the shoppers leave and the gates are closed, fills with jinn who appear toward the end of the night. The guards slip away then, and many's the time I've fought off vicious jinnis and won." He said he was friends with all the families of jinn living there. He also had an extraordinarily beautiful jinni sweetheart named Daldona, who loved him and slept with him on the cloth every night. When I stopped the car near a group of people to ask for Nishan, since I had forgotten the location of his house — or rather his shack — Ifranji added, "This madman, Nishan, won't be any more savage than the jinni named Sherlock, and I cut off his ears and castrated him when he wanted to seduce my girlfriend, Daldona."

I laughed — I needed that laugh — and decided to allow matters to proceed according to my plan. I would not scrap or change a thing — at least not for now.

We climbed out of my car near a group of people standing in front of some carpets spread on the bare ground. Men with diverse miens and of different ages were selling food: bitter black bread, bones with no meat on them, and a few questionable-looking vegetables. The smell of decomposing fish was pervasive. Three women were selling tea and coffee nearby. Everything came to a halt suddenly: the vendors' cries, the importunate bargaining sessions, and the rude courting directed at nubile girls by uncouth tongues. Genuine and insolent curiosity surrounded us as a narrow cordon formed, and a number of children holding small rocks and arrows, supposedly for hunting small birds, approached. But I couldn't see a single green tree – or any tree at all – and where there are no trees there are no birds. Some women whose inquisitiveness had overwhelmed them drew nearer, along with men who resembled Nishan so closely that if I had added lunacy to their résumés and provided them with lit cigarettes and copies of *Hunger's Hopes*, they would all have become Nishan in that novel.

I was approached by a bearded man of about fifty. He was relatively clean and wore garments made of unbleached *dammur* cotton as well as a white turban. He accosted me directly and said that his name was Hajj al-Bayt (or Pilgrim of the Holy House) and that he was the imam of the only mosque in the district.

He pointed to a patch of ground to my left; there wasn't any actual building, only a section of bare land outlined by horizontal rows of mud bricks and pebbles. Inside were spread old kilim carpets with frayed edges. The pulpit seemed to be some old pieces of wood arranged like a dais. He asked me why we were in Wadi al-Hikma and if we were important government representatives who wanted to bring joy to residents' hearts with good news. They had, it seemed, been waiting for the arrival of water and electrical service for some time

78

and yearned to receive titles to the tracts on which they lived.

Ifranji and I aroused suspicion because we obviously didn't belong there. I doubt that the hand of a government that brings delight to hearts is long enough to extend to such a district. The hand that will arrive is the other one, the brutal hand that tears down cardboard and corrugated metal shacks and evicts residents to points unknown. I told the man that we weren't from the government and brought no news. We were merely looking for Nishan Hamza Nishan, who lived there, for an important matter.

"Nishan Hamza Nishan? This is odd. No one has asked for him for a long time. Do you know him?" he asked. "What do you want with him?"

He seemed to think our mission eccentric, and the group that clustered around us ever more tightly did too. The skeletons of unfinished houses, the shacks of corrugated metal and the little piles of human excrement in the empty lots of a district that totally lacked storm sewers left me incredulous. No one would actually request a lunatic distinguished only by his poverty in such a poor district. A novelist who had received seventy folded pages from this man telepathically was fully justified, however, in making such a request on behalf of his conscience. The novelist's conscience made the request, not the novelist.

"We wish to treat his schizophrenia," I explained as I attempted to show with my very posture how serious we were. With hands clasped behind my back, I looked the man straight in the eye, although Joseph Ifranji had adopted

79

a loafer's classic pose. He had removed his broken sunglasses and begun to stare with lustful eyes at a brown girl who was about twenty and appeared to be a Southerner attracted by the all-encompassing curiosity.

"Treat him?" Hajj al-Bayt asked.

I had paid no attention to his strange name; in other circumstances I would have been immensely interested and would have considered using this name for a character that would resemble him, because I had never before heard of a man named Hajj al-Bayt. I would never have thought that anyone had this name – and that's exactly what happened when I blindly wrote down the name Nishan. I had been enchanted by my sweet discovery, even though it now seemed that I actually hadn't discovered it. The imam's voice had become a rabble-rouser's. He raised his hands on high, revealing the stubble of white armpit hair that had been plucked, and started off, as if in a pulpit, "Why should you treat him? In exchange for what? Suhayla Ahmadu went mad years before he did and ate dogs and cats. No one treated her. Nurayn Hamidayn, a proper tailor, went insane and walked naked in the street, shaking his genitals, but no one treated him. This young man, Murtaja, was studying at the university and went mad. Now he declares confidently that he is Wikipedia – the free encyclopedia – and that in his head are a billion pages on which the entire world is written. Yet we haven't heard of anyone trying to treat him."

Murtaja was barefoot, his gray shirt had lost its buttons, and the hems of his shorts were frayed. He paced back and forth, speaking nonstop while gazing down at the ground. At that moment he was reciting a random page from the Wikipedia of his unbalanced mind. It was devoted to Nasnusa, a creature that ate human flesh and that had defeated the mighty Roman army in the Battle of Wadi al-Hikma. Murtaja walked by Ifranji without looking up. He paused, stopped his recitation of the entry for Nasnusa, and verbally attacked the Southerner, who was still trying to court the brown girl, with an entry devoted to passion and passionate lovers, beginning a year before the Nativity.

A writer's persona seized hold of me briefly as I recognized that this peripheral neighborhood was a trove for creative writing. I might return here to build a corrugated metal hovel where I would live for a time while I wrote about the entire district.

This would not be out of character for me, because I am used to wading into adventures without thinking twice when writing flames in me or illuminates me with its green light. I once lived in a comparable district and served time in prison; I went into business with a woman named Amina Sarmadu to distill liquor from sorghum and dates when I wanted to write a novel that featured a female vendor of these locally brewed beverages.

Unfortunately, the writer's persona did not linger in my mind for long. It self-destructed when Hajj al-Bayt continued bombastically, "You haven't told me why you're interested in Nishan. First of all: who are you? Nishan we know. We know about his insanity that comes and goes. We even know how dangerous he can be. For us, though, he is not a big problem. Either help us achieve a better standard of living or leave us in peace."

I was about to interrupt to clarify the situation for this man, who seemed capable of understanding my motivations if I explained them more fully, when an old geezer started shouting. He wore a patched green loin cloth and was leaning on the shoulder of a girl of about seven. She might have been his granddaughter or that of any other sheikh his age, because I know that in these districts, paternity isn't limited to one's actual father – men play father to their own children and all the other kids.

"God is most great! Down with the villains! Down with the traitors! Glory and honor to the people of the fatherland!"

This ill-timed cry from the elderly man, who was as old as Abd al-Qawi but lacked the Shadow's wisdom and talent, was a senile outburst with consequences that I had not wanted or expected when I set out in search of Nishan Hamza. We hadn't come as villains and weren't enemies of the state. An enemy of the proletariat does not come searching for one of them.

I realized then that I found myself in a serious crisis that was growing more dangerous with every passing moment.

Why had I listened at all to Nishan Hamza? Why had I brought him, eyes closed and bewildered, into my spiritual mother's home and allowed him to speak? Why hadn't I acted like some damn writer who creates ivory towers for himself and recruits an arrogant guard force to repel problems like Nishan – without the author having to know about it? I could have signed a copy of the novel for him at the Social Harmony Club and laughed or felt sad for a few moments or fled to my car – without waiting for him. He would never have come across me when I was alone, and at any other time the people surrounding me would have stopped him from ending my life. In fact, I myself could easily have escaped from him but hadn't.

"*Allahu Akbar!* Down with all who betray the people!"

Voices assailed us as the ring around us tightened threateningly. Then the imam, Hajj al-Bayt, whether on purpose or because he had no other choice, finally sided with us and used his voice at its maximum strength to stop the mayhem. He made it clear that we intended no harm to anyone in Wadi al-Hikma and that we were benevolent souls who actually had come to treat a son of the district. He could have said this at first, when harmony reigned supreme, but hadn't. He could have prolonged that harmony, but hadn't.

The angry talk eventually calmed in response to the imam's appeal, and the circle began to loosen. Selling resumed from rags spread on the ground, and buying perked up too. Hajj al-Bayt, the imam, insisted on accompanying us in person on our expedition to track down Nishan.

We didn't find him in his shack, which contained a worn-out mat, a dirty *dammur* cotton pillow from which soiled stuffing protruded, a number of tunics and turbans that were tossed here and there, and many books. These must have been law books for his legal studies, which had been suspended. I also glimpsed some ragdolls and shuddered.

We didn't discover him at any of the construction sites teeming with workers, even though he had occasionally worked as a day laborer. That ceased, however, when he was no longer able to work.

The indefatigable Hajj al-Bayt climbed out of my car whenever it came to a stop. He would enter a house and pop back out. Finally he was obliged to accompany us to an outlying section of the district with seven mud-brick houses, which he said were filthy and of bad repute. Ethiopian women lived there, and he didn't know whether Nishan visited them or not. Our fugitive, however, wasn't there either.

Finally we discovered him on an abandoned section of railroad track. In the past, this line had carried passengers and freight from the port to the capital, but fast, modern, paved roads had rendered it obsolete.

Nishan had reached one of the extreme stages of his schizophrenia. He was wearing the torn uniform of a general and drilling seven adolescent boys. Apparently to punish them for being mutinous soldiers who had fled from a battle, he had lined them up, single file. Their posture in the line showed that they thought the whole affair was a big joke.

Suddenly, as we approached, Nishan abandoned his military reserve and threw a boy to the ground and knelt on

84

his belly. He and the boy were yelling, but the other boys continued to mock him. Joseph Ifranji, Hajj al-Bayt, and I rushed to them and helped the teenagers lift Nishan from the boy's belly. We threw him in the back seat of the car. Joseph Ifranji bound Nishan's feet and hands with a stout rope he pulled from beneath his seat, trussing him up brilliantly. Ifranji repeated, "I knew I would need you, rope. Thanks, Rope!"

Nishan yielded more completely than I would ever have imagined possible. At critical moments like this he seemed incapable of inspiring a novel or of transmitting one by telepathy. He also seemed a lover unlikely to have captivated an educated nurse. He did not seem to be an ordinary Wadi al-Hikma loafer who bought supplies from a carpet spread on the ground.

As we were preparing to depart with our disturbed catch, I asked Hajj al-Bayt, "Doesn't Nishan have some family members or relatives here?"

"No," he replied. "Not here — but there are definitely some elsewhere. He used to have a relative here named Zakariya, a truck driver who hauled brick and gravel to construction sites. He disappeared last year, and people say he married an Ethiopian girl and went with her to her country."

He had a relative who drove a truck? My God! I had included him as a character in *Hunger's Hopes* too — the trucker who calmed Nishan down when he became hysterical. He would tie him up with ropes whenever he sensed that Nishan was becoming dangerous.

Hajj al-Bayt asked me, "Where are you taking him?"

"To a psychiatric hospital," I replied as we departed.

By then day had ebbed away, and a desolate, depressing night was preparing to claim Wadi al-Hikma.

– 9 –

I SAT IN THE OFFICE of Dr Shakir, the head of al-Nakhil Private Psychiatric Hospital. Three buttons had popped off my shirt and my hair had become disheveled during our struggle with Nishan. I smelled embarrassingly rank from sweat and was in a hurry to return home to attend to myself physically and mentally and restore to myself some of the dignity that had evaporated in a struggle I should have avoided. The only link between this conflict and myself was a silly story called *Hunger's Hopes*.

I had begun to hate the novel intensely. I hoped that no further copies would be sold and that its distribution would be limited to the copies already sold. If I could find a way to collect all the remaining copies from the warehouses, I would. The Shadow had asserted with total confidence and arrogance that Nishan had sent it to me and himself fiddled with the parts that did not correspond to his life. That made me merely the recipient; I had received this catastrophe and made things considerably worse. The Shadow, however, had ignored many things, such as my style, which hasn't changed from one story to another. He had ignored my technique, which I claim to have invented, of playing around with sections and chronology. I put one step in the place of

87

another that originally preceded it and delay the arrival of one word out of respect for another. These are all my own tricks that I am sure could not have turned up in a telepathic text. The Shadow was swayed by his relationship with Father Matthew and by his claim that the play wasn't one he had created. I, for my part, was still wavering and unable to reach any conclusion, whether sagacious or fallacious.

What I had written down had actually happened. I had simply added a future I wanted to happen. Had Nishan been responsible for the entire story, there would have been no possibility of the character dying of glandular cancer. He was timorous and did not want to die. That was patently clear.

I realized that I was attempting to analyze matters that defied analysis and was thus taxing my mind pointlessly. The psychiatrist opposite me was elegant and rather handsome, even though he was getting on in years. Dr Shakir was a longtime friend, a classmate from secondary school. In my opinion, he could have had a successful career as a singer. He had encouraged us to listen to songs and had occasionally sung himself. He drew satirical caricatures, but only a few people knew about this talent.

When we brought Nishan from Wadi al-Hikma to the hospital, he was in no state to be lodged in an ordinary house overnight in anticipation of an examination by a specialist in the morning. We transported him in the car – tormented and rather disgusting. He struggled against the rope's constraints, attempted to escape, succeeding to some degree and frightening Ifranji, who now doubted his prior conviction that he could guard Nishan and serve as his paid caregiver.

I watched as Ifranji, this self-styled conqueror of the jinn and heart-throb of Daldona, turned in alarm, scratching his skimpy beard with dirty fingers. I heard him tell me I needed to speed up. Then, in his own special whisper, in a barely audible voice, he lauded the torn rag he had stretched out on every night in the Aisha Market, before I had tracked him down and hired him for this nightmare.

Ifranji's demeanor suggested that he would bow out of this assignment, and I didn't want to pressure him further, in order to prevent him from fleeing my embrace. I needed him for many services. It crossed my mind at that moment that I should give him the rental house and tell him candidly that it would be for Nishan, once he was cured.

When I first hired Ifranji, I had not told him about the telepathy tale that had shaken me and led to my involvement with Nishan Hamza, because I knew he would never fathom a cursed mystery like this. He knew me as a former math teacher in the school where he had once worked as an errand boy; he had quit when I did. He knew I was currently a writer with no day job, but his limited cultural background and his defective knowledge of the language in which I write had prevented him from reading any of my works. In fact, I doubt he would have read them even if he had been fully literate and fluent in Arabic.

At the time I had told him, "I'm performing my duty as a human being on behalf of an individual whose family

I know." For his part, he had only asked about Nishan's syndrome and his mercurial personality.

We brought Nishan — or NHN as I thought of him, because his lengthy name had started to oppress and depress me whenever I uttered it or even thought about it — to the hospital. He was still tormented by his symptoms and struggling with Ifranji's strong rope. He was also cursing at a mutinous soldier in the army he had created on the abandoned railroad line, a lazy wastrel of a fly that wouldn't let him sleep, and a damned boy named Adula, who called him with a feminine voice and wouldn't stop. Even the drowsiest eyes turned to look when we passed on the streets or stopped at a red light. En route I told Dr Shakir by phone about Nishan's tragedy and mine. His understanding of schizophrenia was keen, but he did not wish to wade into a discussion with me about telepathy, either because he considered it an urban myth or because he didn't understand it.

Nishan was received at the door of the hospital the way non compos mentis patients usually are. They used strong leather straps to fasten him to a clean stretcher and then carried him to an isolated room, where not even a trifling fly was allowed access without written permission.

I observed him stretched out on a white metal bed with his wrists manacled or lying on the table next to him. I watched him as he calmed down and fell asleep. Occasional snot dripped from his nose, but his insane slobbering had stopped. Then, if a dream toyed with him, it was inevitably a rosy one that featured his departed but beloved Ranim or a rowdy courtroom with defendants and witnesses at whom he barked instructions, because he was the judge.

Joseph Ifranji, who had clipped his shades to his shirt pocket once night fell, roamed the hospital in search of nurses who had left the South. He hoped to detain them long enough for some fleeting romance, as he informed me. I gave him several pounds and offered him a choice between sleeping in the small rental house or returning to the Aisha Market where he usually lived, loitered, and hugged Daldona, daughter of the jinn. He chose the house – not because he thought it superior, as he informed me, but because his jinni lover was out of town for the time being. She had traveled with her family to a desert resort where they spent their summer holidays each year.

By my lights, this Ifranji is a unique character and deserves – with his broken Arabic and the tales he tells without cracking a smile or laughing – to be the protagonist of a novel. I have already mentioned that I once appropriated his character. That was, unfortunately, buried in an abandoned manuscript that I believe will never see the light of day. I was happy to rediscover him, and the fact that he had named his son after a tree that he had heard about by chance in the market inspired many paragraphs that I could use in future works. This, however, wasn't the time for writing. First, someone needed to crack the multifaceted riddle that was NHN.

I asked Dr Shakir, who had filled his fancy pipe with tobacco but not lit it, for his personal analysis of Nishan's condition and whether he could be cured and become a judge as he hoped.

I was searching for a cigarette to light but found none in my pocket. The doctor set his pipe on the table and replied without any of the circumspection that is common in such situations, "It's true that his schizophrenia is seasonal and intermittent and that when he takes Risperdal or Haloperidol regularly, all his symptoms disappear. But he's unfit to be a judge, a court official, or even a humble court messenger."

I felt that his opinion was a fatal blow to Nishan's ambitions. The question of studying law was moot; it would be a long time before he became a normal human being and escaped from the death that awaited him at the end of my novel.

Once I returned to my house, I realized that I had been so caught up in the succession of untoward events that I hadn't slept even momentarily for two days. I discovered that my mobile phone had been turned off most of the time since I left the home of Malikat al-Dar, my spiritual mother, accompanied by Nishan. I had only thought of turning it on during the minutes I spoke to Dr Shakir. I had turned it off again afterwards. There would certainly be dozens of calls and text messages; the callers and message-senders would have no idea what had happened to me or would happen.

A number of my friends would certainly have wondered what my secret reason was for turning off my phone. Some of them would surely have thought I had traveled again, after spending no more than a day in my homeland – without informing anyone. When I realized that some might have thought I had died, leaving my decomposing corpse in my house, I feared they might try to track me down in any manner they could think of. Just as I expected, when I turned on my phone, I found more than twenty messages. Most were from literary colleagues, and a number of these concerned the meeting they had had today at the working-class coffeehouse called al-Muzira, where we usually met. There was also a message from a journalist with a local newspaper, because I had scheduled a long interview with him for today about my detestable novel *Hunger's Hopes*. I had stood him up. I doubted that I would keep any future appointments concerning that novel.

Najma had also texted me and wanted me to call her the moment I received her message. She had not, however, mentioned why she was contacting me. She had left that vague. The message that most gripped me, though, was from Linda, the daughter of Abd al-Qawi the Shadow – or the Shadow's shadow, as I thought of her. Linda was a strange girl. I had never seen her in person, although I had been in her father's residence dozens of times over a period of many years, even before she was born. I had never seen her at a lecture, cultural event, performance of one of her father's plays, or in the market or a gloomy or brilliant alley anywhere in the world. When her name came up or she was mentioned in passing, the Shadow spoke of her proudly. He was the one who had given her my cell number which she had used to forge a strong telephone friendship with me.

She shared with me opinions she had formed about works she read by many different writers and about all my works, which she said she enjoyed reading. She also discussed her own projects, which included a novel she called *Two Wheels and Body Parts*. She had been busy writing this for the past two years, and eventually it would be published. She had not told me what her novel was about, and I had never asked. I repeatedly invited her to the lectures I gave or to parties I was attending, but she had always declined without offering a convincing reason.

Her voice on the telephone was quite distinctive. It was the voice of a girl dreaming or discussing the remnants of a dream she was clinging to, hoping it wouldn't escape. Some sentences were fresh and succulent. Half her words were clear and half somewhat hard to grasp. There was a delicate breathiness to her speech, and the hint of a laugh resonated through it from time to time.

In fact, Linda the Shadow had frequently whetted my imagination. I had attempted to picture her, based on what I knew about her. I had come up with a mental portrait of her as a girl of twenty or thereabouts, slender, with lively eyes, soft skin, and full, black hair trimmed with colorful ribbons. Her head swayed gently when she walked. I felt an odd curiosity to verify my portrait and said to the Shadow one evening when we sat in his house, trying to make my words seem innocent and unpremeditated, "Master, Linda is a cultural icon. She reads everything I write and offers me her frank opinion even about works by other authors. Why doesn't she participate in our cultural activities or at least come occassionally to sit with us and join our conversations?'

I noticed his expression changed slightly, as if he had not liked what he heard or had indigestion. Then he replied, "What a lovely idea, Writer! Linda actually is a perceptive scholar. Her problem is that she cannot handle other people."

Then his narrow eyes drilled into my face, and he added, "It should suffice for her to converse with you by phone. Isn't that so? You know what she thinks of your works and of ones by other authors. I don't think you want to marry her – isn't that so?"

Thinking that I had caused trouble by asking about Linda, I moved our conversation in a direction that I knew the Shadow would relish enough to erase any problem or discomfort. I started discussing his play *A Day in the Lantimaru Garden*, which was a brilliant dramatic fantasy about an imaginary day spent with a dinosaur in a garden called Lantimaru, somewhere beyond the Earth's sphere.

I mentioned that Linda's message had attracted my feverish attention. Long and eloquently phrased, it discussed *Hunger's Hopes*, which she had just finished reading, in a delightful fashion. She asked me about the ending: "Did you have to torture Nishan Hamza so excruciatingly? You could have aimed a treacherous bullet from an unknown assailant to strike him in the neck or run over him with a speeding car when he was crossing a street paved with death."

In an essay that I wrote about anxious reading, published a year and a half ago in a newspaper, and posted on a website that I write for occasionally, I discussed the mechanics of producing a novel and of receiving it. I said a writer works with limits he determines with help from scrupulous observers. These include his talent, knowledge, and expertise, and an internal overseer that forms in his mind and that supersedes it. Thus he writes without looking at anything. If something happens and his thinking becomes confused or miscarries for some reason, this will never be a false step. He observes this miscarriage, and his vision extends forward, as he attempts to set his other thoughts on their own two feet. Consequently, Nishan Hamza, or NHN, must die of glandular cancer. Any other outcome a reader suggests would stem from temporary sympathy for the character, not from profound digging in the dirt of writing.

Linda was an excellent reader – there was no doubt about that. The overly literary sentences describing the hero's death must have infuriated her. My ending was unexpected, because the invalid doesn't die of complications of his schizophrenia. Her suggestion, however, was well off the mark.

I replied quickly to her message, realizing that she might be waiting up to receive my response. I clarified my thinking for her and directed her attention to my essay for further guidance.

Another text message really made me laugh. It was from Joseph Ifranji, who must have loaded his phone with credit when I gave him money. He had written in his idiosyncratic English: "My lover Daldona return back from the desert. She discovered the rented house and now with me in the bed."

I can at this point add something to what I have always asserted. Whenever I have observed Ifranji, listened to him in person, received his texts, or heard his voice on my phone, I have been certain that thanks to him I possess a living novel that is growing in my life and that will emerge as an actual novel one day.

The final serious message was from a friend who works in the Ministry of the Interior, in the division dealing with identity cards. Quite early today, before I went to see Abd al-Qawi the Shadow, I had sent him an email with some brief information about Nishan. His reply confirmed that the man's statements tallied with his files and that the ID he carried had actually been issued more than seven years ago.

Now all I had to do was to keep tabs on this schizophrenic in al-Nakhil Hospital and focus on part of my life that I had neglected for the last two days. I turned off my phone again without calling Najma to find out what she wanted. Accompanied by my insomnia, I strode into my bedroom, where insomnia gradually faded away. The next morning when I awoke I discovered that I had slept soundly without tossing and turning or brooding. I smelled food cooking and heard the vacuum cleaner vibrating the floor of my house. Umm Salama was here, resolutely tidying up my unruly bachelor life.

I sat down at my table and turned on my computer. I went to Facebook to see what had been added during my brief absence, because there was always something new. I read with little interest the commentary on my last entry, which was the word "telepathy". By quickly perusing the new photos Najma had posted that morning, I discovered a love poem, which was fragmentary and monstrous, from an admirer who called himself "The Afflicted Moon". I also found an article by me about the rise to power of religious factions – the reasons for them and their implications; it had appeared on the op-ed page of one of the newspapers.

The Virtuous Sister's page, which I thought of as the treasure-trove page, was full of booby traps, and the number of visitors had increased significantly from the day before. The Anti-Christ was lamenting the delay in the end of the world. The Mobile Charger was bewailing the scarcity of electricity. The person claiming to be "The Yearning, Choking Sheikh" had posted a new love poem that was not available to everyone; again he requested an email. The fellow who referred to himself as "Dead Man" had written: "We are God's and to Him we return."

The Virtuous Sister's friends were fighting ferociously among themselves, and she appeared only as a full stop, a delicate question mark, or not at all. She had removed her picture in a black veil and replaced it with one showing her wearing the same type of niqab but in gray.

My personal email account was overflowing with messages; I didn't open them because I was afraid they might bring new crises. I already was dealing with a crisis with consequences I hadn't been able to handle.

I turned off the computer and grabbed my copy of *Hunger's Hopes*, quickly turning to the page after the one that had been folded over. There I read about the mental hospital, an injected tranquilizer, and an intravenous drip that induced a tranquil state. I read about Yaqutah the nurse who worked in the hospital and who couldn't keep herself from crying at work for the patient she had been fond of for a year and still was attached to. She didn't know if this was true love or merely human sympathy that had grown in her and she could not shake off. I read about the flood of feelings in the filthy ward, which housed multiple patients with a variety of mental ailments. They were shouting, screaming, weeping, laughing, and attempting in rare moments of lucidity to escape from the intense surveillance and allow their savage illnesses the freedom to cross-pollinate in the streets.

By the end of the page, Nishan had begun to recover, becoming more lucid. He was able to remember Wadi al-Hikma and his beloved nurse's face. His normal excuses were able to form in his mind, and he would definitely share them with everyone he had exposed to the fallout from his delirium, wherever he had acted out of control.

Nishan's bout of insanity and confinement to a hospital were true to life, but Yaqutah, the nurse who had emigrated and changed her name to Ranim, was missing. The real hospital was clean, not filthy, and people with many types of mental illnesses were not crowded together in one ward. Nishan was actually lying in a clean room in a private hospital, and I was definitely paying for all his expenses. Even if Dr Shakir was a friend and very accommodating and sympathetic, the language of the bottom line supplanted all other tongues.

I had no intention of visiting Nishan that day or any other unless there was a sudden change in his condition. I was content with what I had done for him to date and felt no need for a visit. The most that I would try to do in the future was to wait for his complete cure and release from the hospital. Then I would attempt to have him checked for glandular cancer – to determine whether he actually had it or whether the real-life version of the text rectified this part as it had many other passages.

I sensed that my life had become unsettled and that what had happened in just two days was unprecedented during all the years of my adult life, part of which I had spent teaching math and part of which I had killed myself writing those asinine novels. If I asked myself now what actual profit a novel like *Hunger's Hopes* could achieve, balanced against its enormous losses, I would say I had actually made no profit at all. I was on the verge of going stark raving mad myself and tearing up my two remaining copies of the novel. I regained control of myself only when one of them was about to be shredded.

I would not allow a crisis like this to cause me to abandon writing quite so easily. To become a writer I had abandoned a profession that was not merely respectable but also somewhat equitable in terms of providing me a living wage and a woman whom I loved and who loved me. In retrospect, teaching may have been the better option when the choice was presented as between house and the lady of the house – and writing.

I turned on my phone in order to reclaim my normal day and in keeping with my latest decision. I was surprised by the noisy rings of Najma's call even before my phone was fully on.

– *10* –

THE SIGHT BEFORE ME now was totally unfamiliar. I sensed I was confronting a different girl from the Najma I had met back in the days of "The Neighbors' Goat" and during the subsequent period of quarrels and reconciliation, of brief meetings I felt she had rehearsed in advance. This young woman exuded grace – from her stylish clothes and splendid smile to the glances of a precisely delineated femininity, which I had never, ever, expected from her.

That morning Dr Shakir had phoned me to say that Nishan had improved considerably but would need to remain for a number of additional days under medical supervision. Then he would be able to return to his normal life. In brief, there was no need for me to interrupt my busy schedule to come see him.

That was what I had decided with total satisfaction to do before the doctor called. Joseph Ifranji had also informed me by the "single ring" or, as I referred to it, the "I need you but have no credit" method, that living in the rental house in a working-class neighborhood had greatly helped his nerves. He was hoping that his wife, Ashul, would return with their son, Mahogany, from the new state of South Sudan to share his delightful dwelling. Daldona, his jinni

102

girlfriend from the Aisha Market, had become angry for no reason at all and left him. He didn't think she would return, not even if he went back to the torn rag in that clamorous market. He added that he had met some neighbors who were pleasant and companionable, including a drunkard with a fine singing voice, a woman who made excellent syrup-soaked *zalabiya* doughnuts, and a professional demonstrator against the ruling elite; he was usually in prison or about to be returned there. The activist's name was Sallum, but in the district his nickname was Beauty Spot. He, Joseph Ifranji, was seriously considering changing his name to Beauty Spot so he would be known as Beauty Spot Ifranji, because he was deeply impressed by this stalwart man. I laughed wholeheartedly and told him that Beauty Spot Ifranji would be a troublesome, offensive name ill-suited to the miserable life he was leading. In fact, the authorities might arrest him for it and deport him to his country. I knew that Ifranji would never be convinced. He had long been accustomed to changing his name as circumstances arose only to return later to his original name. He was once Joseph Mandela and then Joseph Bin Laden, along with other names I no longer recalled. During what was approximately the hour left before I was to meet Najma, I leafed through a book on the science of the paranormal, searching for something that would help me solve the riddle posed by Nishan and *Hunger's Hopes*. Unfortunately I found nothing significant. It was an unpretentious recital of Sufi miracles, such as crossing the sea without boats, being physically present in two different places at the same time, and turning plain water into milk, without any explanation of the mechanics of these feats. I abandoned that book with the intention of searching for another more useful one and left for my appointment with Najma.

Najma had arrived before me and was waiting for me, seated at a comfortable table in the Juwana Café in the affluent Al-Riyadh neighborhood. She wore a light blue blouse – in a modern style, for the first time – and a black satin skirt. Her gray silk headscarf matched her outfit, and many changes were visible on her face. She had applied eye shadow and eyelash extensions, and plucked her eyebrows till they were as narrow as a thread.

She was, in brief, a modern girl – something she hadn't wanted to be throughout those past years – and a dutiful slave to fashion.

I found myself gazing at her even before I greeted her. My conjectures raced breathlessly to explore her psychological depths, wishing to guess what had happened and what might happen now.

Without reflecting whether it was an appropriate question, I asked, "What's happened? Why have you changed so suddenly?"

She tilted her head slightly to the left in a familiar and deliberately flirtatious movement that women frequently resort to, but did not smile. She replied, "I want to become a mother."

My next question also popped out without any reflection or consideration of whether it was suitable. "Have you married? Who is it? Your friend Tulumba?"

She choked up, no doubt about it, and frowned severely. "Would I marry someone like Tulumba? Are you serious? In any case, Tulumba has passed into God's care, may God have mercy on his soul."

I was as thunderstruck as if she had mentioned one of my relatives or friends. "Has Hamid Tulumba really died?"

"Yes . . . Six months ago, in one of those traffic accidents we witness every day. So the novel he was writing for my life was lost."

I didn't know what to say when this supercilious girl was supercilious even about a tragedy and spoke of her wretched lover's death as if she were discussing the death of a repulsive cockroach in a corner of her kitchen. What had interested her about his existence was how he was "writing" a role for her as a legendary beloved, even as she progressed step by step through an ordinary life. She had been seeking inspiration from the pages that his life created for a silly, boring novel, one I doubt she could have written. Otherwise, why had she once asked me to write it?

I began wrestling with myself about whether I should remain there with her to investigate her newfound femininity and the causes for it or return to my own life and purify it of this cruelty by mourning for a miserable boy. I hadn't really known Tulumba well, but I could imagine the life he might have lived had he loved a girl other than Najma.

At that moment Tulumba won out, and I rose while the coffee the elegant waiter had brought was still hot and untouched. Najma, however, grasped my hand entreatingly, and I sensed then that her hand belied her persona. This was a tender woman's hand. She said, "Please sit down. Please, Master."

I sat back down, disgruntled, and she began to speak at once. "Forget the past, Master. Tell me frankly: Why didn't you remarry after your divorce seven years ago?"

This was an unexpected question, and the girl had prepped herself on my biography. I had dozens of answers I could regurgitate. I could tell her, for example, that marriage is antithetical to creative writing or — more accurately — is injurious to it. I could say that a creator who is preoccupied by the thrust of creation cannot exert a comparable thrust on behalf of his family. I could inform her that the presence of books in a conjugal home is comparable to the presence of land mines in a small field: they may explode and create chaos, provoking quarrels any day. I could say that my life belonged to me and that I cared for it; it allowed me to roam when I occasionally needed to in order to produce a manuscript.

But I said nothing of the kind. I gripped the staff by the middle merely to learn what was passing through her cruel mind and what her new femininity concealed. I don't know; I simply wasn't thinking. "The failure of the first experiment perhaps caused me to avoid repeating it."

"Possibly," she responded as her head inclined to the right and a lock of hair, dyed dark brown, peeked out boldly from beneath her gray scarf.

"Possibly, but not all experiments are the same. Even in your narrative experiments, you certainly must have had successful experiments and others that were less so. Do you agree with me?"

I undoubtedly agreed with her. There certainly were novels I wished I hadn't written, especially when I was first starting out and was stingy with my narration. I would pursue the rhythm of the sentences breathlessly. I didn't exploit some characters well; others I exploited in an exaggerated way, leaving them anemic. I had been candid in my reading of my personal experiments and greeted whatever was worth greeting in them wholeheartedly and blamed harshly whatever was blameworthy. I had striven industriously for many years to track down the maladies and defects in my writing's corpus so I could treat them. Perhaps I have succeeded at that; perhaps I have failed. In any case, experimentation ultimately remains the author's child, to be adopted willingly or not.

"Yes, I agree with you, but why are you asking these strange questions?"

I realized as I contemplated her more and recalled my meetings with her that I had never written about a character like this and that there would be no harm in my writing about such a person – I mean a woman who is awed by her own ideas and focuses only on them, who can exploit ugliness and transform it into beauty. Thus she sees the tortured moans of people harmed by her as disturbing her peace of mind, whereas her own moan is like a colored light that other people should be dazzled by and follow. Even cruel Salma, the police officer who made innovations in sexual torture and about whom I wrote in one of my novels — I have mentioned that I prolonged her life in the last two pages to allow her a chance to apologize to her numerous victims before she died — was, in the final analysis, a woman convinced that she was in a field of work that ended when the work day did. She would return home, embrace her husband, kiss her child, and light the stove to cook dinner. Najma was totally different; Najma was a one of a kind character. I swear that she had never swept a dusty courtyard, had never washed a dirty dish, and had never even turned off an alarm clock when she woke up. Now she aspired — in a frivolous manner — to assume the status of mother while lacking all the aptitudes.

But what man would grant her this honor?

I sensed genuine distress when I considered that she might want to marry me personally. If not, what was the point of these changes that she had adopted when meeting me? Why was she asking me about marriage at precisely this moment? I had known her for quite some time and she had never asked such questions before.

I forced myself to shake off my despair while I waited to hear what she would say.

"In short . . ." Najma replied as many burdens vanished from her face to be replaced by new gentle attractions. Two locks of her brown hair were now in clear view, and her breathing seemed more regular. A decorative fish tank stood on a shelf within my field of view, and it seemed to me that a sparkling fish inside it was swimming with a vanity quite unlike that of the other fish.

"In short, after profound thought and after sifting through all the men I know, whether or not they have proposed to marry me, I have chosen you to be my husband and grant me motherhood. It wouldn't hurt you. I don't claim that I would make you happy or compensate you for your former life, but I have an intense need to become a mother."

I was not astonished, nor should I have been; this was the type of conduct that fit exactly the character I knew. Even if Najma hadn't said that, I would have invented it myself and attributed it to her character, without any hesitation or sense that I was violating a woman's rights.

This was the first time I had heard of a girl who wanted to marry in order to be fertilized. She would no doubt be the last, unless I was unlucky enough to meet other Najmas who carried the same germ.

When I inevitably first became acquainted with women and met a woman whom I loved and who loved me, a woman I married (even though we later quarreled), I met a female who bore the transparent inheritance of females. She would have felt it inappropriate to employ even her glances to express a desire. Now, feeling indisposed, I was confronted by a weird mannequin, but I would escape from her clutches.

I would not marry a girl who had devised for the late petition writer painful roads to follow till he died. I actually wouldn't even contemplate marrying her.

The Juwana Café had begun to fill with young guys with long hair, ripped jeans, and shirts with pictures of the wrestler John Cena on them. They turned off the lights without permission or justification and lit colored candles on all the tables, even the table where I sat with Najma. I didn't grasp the point of this until the coffeehouse was rocked by music that shattered my head and nerves. I decided that I had to terminate our meeting and terminate Najma, knowing she wouldn't consider this a defeat and would endeavor to transform our abortive meeting into a flimsy victory that only she would be able to brag about.

11

D URING THE TWO WEEKS after Najma upset me in the Juwana Café, I realized, for the first time in seven years, that I actually needed a woman, although definitely not Najma – because I considered her a scary nightmare, and that was the end of that – but some other woman I might seek once my life, which had been total chaos ever since Nishan appeared to throw that damn book at me and to cling to my neck, calmed down.

Without knowing it, Najma had drawn my attention to Umm Salama, the widow who attempted to straighten me out and tidy up my house, preparing food for me twice a week. She wasn't really an excellent or a half-way proficient worker, and even her cooking wasn't great or healthy. Her washing and ironing of my clothes were the worst I had experienced, and she always seemed in a rush. She complained about her adolescent sons and their costly dreams whenever she found me in the living room or knocked on the door of my bedroom to ask me something.

Najma had also alerted me to my emotional need for at least a minimal love interest suitable for a heart the age of mine. I hadn't smelled fragrant incense from an ornamental brazier for ages. I hadn't glimpsed a ribbed perfume flask or one shaped like a rose or a serpent – from Coco Chanel, Nina Ricci, or Yves St Laurent – leap from its repose on the dressing-table to a live body I could touch. I hadn't seen new curtains at a window, an elegant comb, a hairdryer, or any other accessory related to beauty or enjoyment. I had been navigating a narrow corridor from uninterrupted dullness to uninterrupted dullness, from creative isolation to limited relaxation to seclusion again. I would write those erroneous novels that did not react against or link to an experience that might be more enriching if my life were better.

I shall no doubt curse Najma for making me notice the death I have been dying while assuming it was a life. I will write about her one day with cramps more severe than those that killed the wretched petition writer Hamid Tulumba.

Suddenly Linda the Shadow came to mind. Actually she herself did not come to mind; rather, it was the brilliant portrait I had worked hard to draw of her, guided by her breathy voice, as delicate as a whisper, and the warm compassion I felt surging from my phone whenever I spoke with her. I summoned the full portrait to my mind and began to regard it with intoxication.

Why shouldn't I aspire to marry Linda the Shadow?

That might prove sheer insanity. I had never seen her and did not know the shape of her face or the look of her eyes. Was she as splendid as I had portrayed her or was she just a girl who read a lot and lacked any other traits that would justify a romantic adventure? Another insane aspect of this project was that I was at least twenty-seven years older, but that was definitely not a problem.

The girl who did not like face-to-face meetings, who did not appear anywhere that curiosity, cameras, or eyes were active, would perhaps prove an astonishing prize for a man so accustomed to confrontations that he could train a butterfly to stand still to confront the light.

Why not really? Linda the Shadow loved my writing and her opinions delighted me. Perhaps she loved me too and was waiting for me. I didn't think the Shadow would reject having a writer for a son-in-law, since he himself was one.

I wished to keep this beautiful thought in my mind for the longest time possible, but it escaped, although I knew it would return. I went on Najma's Facebook page to see what she had written since I fled from her brash advances in Juwana Café. As expected, I discovered that she had reworked the defeat and transformed it into a victory. She had posted a picture that clearly displayed her new femininity and was extremely inflammatory. Beneath the photo she had written: "Even if you brought the moon as my dowry, I would ask you for another moon that you created just for me. Then I would annul the marriage." There were as usual a thousand "likes", including mine, which I deliberately added, and a hundred comments. The most remarkable response came from Fattah, a poet known for his extreme generosity in examining web pages run by women and for posting hungry comments on each page. He had written: "Yes, Najma, but I actually possess three moons in my heart and will be happy to present them to you. Then I'll go celebrate the annulment with my friends."

With reference to the riddle that was Nishan, I can say I tried to forget it daily but never did, because Dr Shakir informed me one day, in an urgent exchange, that I needed to meet with him immediately. I thought the man had succumbed and returned to the state of angry stupor once more and committed countless offenses. The situation was quite different, however. When I met the elegant psychiatrist in his office, he told me what was troubling him. During his stay at the hospital, Nishan had met — either in his room or when he roamed in the courtyard and garden — many fellow patients who had recovered or were on the road to recovery. He had established a strong relationship with Tuba, a reclusive football player who was trying to train birds to play ball; Sihli, who was a former ambassador with the Ministry of Foreign Affairs and who had been afflicted with schizophrenia when he was appointed ambassador to Burkina Faso; Abd al-Azim Tataqawi, who had spent forty years in the College of Medicine but hadn't graduated yet; Sallah Aji, who called himself "Bespoke" and who was once a singer of some renown; and other patients who were all schizophrenics or manic-depressives whose conditions had improved to varying degrees. Nishan had goaded them to abandon their former worlds and to share with him his beautiful world in Wadi al-Hikma as soon as they were discharged from this burrow. They seemed convinced and responsive enough to his call that one now refused to meet his family when they visited the hospital, and another told his family candidly that he wasn't related to them.

Seen from my point of view, the situation was phenomenal, because none of those well-to-do patients being treated in this private hospital could survive for even an hour in Wadi al-Hikma, even if they had no psychiatric condition.

I laughed profoundly, but Dr Shakir was not amused. He plunged into a headstrong discussion of the puzzle of schizophrenia, which remains a chronic condition to the end, leaving those afflicted with split personalities. The injections and pills that are prescribed as treatment are actually merely tranquilizers and do not effect a complete cure. He told me about the great danger that would loom over the residents of Wadi al-Hikma if it became a colony for mental patients, even if only for a day, before those patients were rounded up and returned to the hospital.

I did not join him in the gloom that saturated his phrases and asked him to discharge Nishan from the hospital if that was appropriate, because I wanted him for another matter. I would take him some place where all his glands could be checked to learn his chances of dying the way he did at the end of *Hunger's Hopes*. At that moment, however, we received a big surprise. An alarmed nurse came to inform the director that Nishan Hamza could not be found in the hospital. No one knew how this patient had fled or where he had gone.

The psychiatrist, who had grown tense, asked him, "Did any other patient flee with him?"

"No, all the other patients are accounted for," the nurse replied. Then he departed. I was left to contemplate, for some minutes, damnable possibilities that virtually leapt before me.

The worst eventuality would be for Nishan to consider me an enemy and try to do away with me. I realized that what the doctor had said about the possibility that schizo-phrenics would remain ill throughout their lives was true – if not, why would a man who had recovered, or nearly so, flee from what was a dream refuge, compared with his shabby, dirty, corrugated-metal hovel in Wadi al-Hikma?

I wanted to ask if he had received a telephone call from a woman, because an imaginary image of a woman was dancing in my mind: Ranim, who had emigrated and who had once been Yaqutah, might have returned from abroad suddenly in order to live out with us the ending of *Hunger's Hopes*. I actually did ask, but no one knew. The doctor and I staggered through the hospital, questioning the nurses in the wards, the guards at the entries, and some of the patients who might shed some light on the matter. No one knew anything. Nishan had suddenly evaporated from a ward that not even a fly could enter without a permit. He may also have vanished while strolling in the hospital's garden, although patients were also under a guard's super-vision during those hours.

I suddenly sensed that I needed my brother, Muzaffar. I wanted him to disrupt my isolation and my fear of solitude, which I knew would be haunted by various nightmares in the coming nights. I pulled out my phone and spoke to him. He seemed anxious and said he would come right away, taking the first plane he could book a seat on.

12

O<small>N THAT UNFORGETTABLE EVENING</small>, my brother, Muzaffar, and I were unexpected visitors to the home of the venerable playwright Abd al-Qawi the Shadow. The weather had started to moderate somewhat, and splendid breezes wafted past.

My brother had prolonged his unscheduled holiday a little for my sake. He was casually dressed in ordinary jeans and a floral-pattern shirt, but I was very elegant in a black suit, a blue silk shirt, and a dark red necktie, which I had purchased during one of my trips to Europe.

I had come to commit the insane act that I had sworn to carry out after sleepless nights and obsessive thoughts that were as far as possible from Nishan Hamza and instead were racing down another path. I was going to ask for the hand in marriage of Linda the Shadow, feeling confident that the portrait I had created of her could not lie.

The Shadow was reclining on his wooden bed with rope netting in the courtyard of his house, according to a habit unlikely to change, given his age. A stippled glass containing milk stood before him, the medium-size book he had been reading sat in his hands, and metal-rimmed reading glasses were perched on his face.

I suddenly saw Dr Sabir Hazaz, the doctor of reflexology, who was carrying a spiffy black leather bag, emerge from inside the house where Linda doubtless was with her elderly mother and the girl who had slim breasts and curly hair and who might be a relative or merely a servant – I didn't know which. I knew that the Shadow's only son, Luqman, had migrated to America fourteen years earlier and came back occasionally for a limited number of days, during which he wore embroidered shirts and trousers torn at the knees as he sauntered down the streets and through the markets in search of depressing local franchises of "Kentucky Chicken," McDonald's, and "Pizza King," while he cursed the authorities, backwardness, and beggars stationed in the streets. Then he would return to America to complete his hegira. The Shadow had told me once how proud he was of his son, whose name had now evolved into Loco the Shadow or Loco with a Shadow. He was a professional rap artist in a group called The Gliders, which performed in public concerts and political campaigns and had more fans than our country had inhabitants. I actually hadn't heard of this group and knew nothing about the culture of rap music, but didn't debate this and shared the father's delight with good conscience.

Dr Hazaz didn't glance our way and did not even appear to see us. He headed to the door with energetic strides unusual for a man his age. Now I remembered seeing a red Hummer near the place; I hadn't, however, linked it to the reflexologist and definitely hadn't expected to find him here. But I refused to allow myself to be distracted by curiosity about his presence in the Shadow's house, especially when I had a portrait with missing features that I was attempting to complete and was on a romantic mission of supreme importance that could easily end well or badly.

The past few days, during an exhausting trip searching for Nishan Hamza — whom the long arm of the law was also seeking now that al-Nakhil Psychiatric Hospital had lodged a complaint, unnecessarily I thought — I had gone with my brother, Muzaffar, to Wadi al-Hikma, where the tale's ember had ignited and where it had not yet died. Joseph Ifranji, who actually had changed his name to Beauty Spot Ifranji, didn't accompany us, because he had been caught in an unlicensed bar and was currently being tortured in a factional militia's camp and threatened with the disquieting possibility of deportation to South Sudan.

The broker at Nu'man Realty had told me this after Ifranji stopped sending me text messages. He said he hadn't mentioned my name to the authorities as the person who had rented the dwelling where Ifranji had lived to spare me any unnecessary anxiety. I thanked him enthusiastically and gave him back his house. I felt sorry for Joseph, who was helping me plot out future novels, which I could only imagine while he was gone. Perhaps when I roused myself from my anxiety and crises I would try to free him from that ordeal, if I found he was still in the country.

Imam Hajj al-Bayt wasn't present in Wadi al-Hikma this time and actually wasn't to be found in the entire country. Dozens of the people among those congregated around torn scraps of cloth – selling, buying, and haggling but not selling or buying – volunteered that Hajj al-Bayt had finally hit upon the chance of a lifetime and traveled to work as a muezzin in a remote village in the Sultanate of Oman. One of his relatives worked as a teacher in the village and was able to send him a work permit, a snappy outfit, and even a plane ticket on Fly Dubai, a new airline. His children would soon join him there.

I was delighted that a resident of Wadi al-Hikma had graduated to something that was definitely better, even if that meant working on the peak of a mountain or in a barren desert. But at the same time I felt naked, because we now lacked any protection or moral cover should we happen to face a dilemma, like the first time, when a senile old man had raised a cry against us and we were almost throttled by the residents. Nothing like that happened to us this time, fortunately, no circle constricted and widened around us, and no lackluster old man loitered there. Sales from the dirty rags continued unabated, and the pathetic purchasing picked up and slowed down. An old pickup truck of no discernable color was parked there with mounds of watermelons and overly ripe tomatoes in the back. Before we set out on our quest for Nishan, whom no one reported seeing in the district since we had plucked him from it by force that previous time, a rather chic youth, wearing a straw hat and gray necktie that hung down his chest, inside out, asked me if I remembered the young man Murtaja. He had heard from people that I had come to the district once and must have seen him.

My first thought was that the name sounded odd and unfamiliar. But I remembered him all of a sudden. Yes, Murtaja of Wikipedia, the young man who roamed around in torn shorts, staring at the ground while reciting odd stories from the version of the Wikipedia that lived in his head, starting with Nasnusa, who ate the flesh of cats and conquered the Roman army in the battle of Wadi al-Hikma. Yes, that's who he was.

"What's become of him? Don't tell me he emigrated with the imam?" Not wanting to respond to his question, I asked him this. My question seemed innocent enough, because it would be unusual for a person whose intellect had left him to leave the country. Murtaja lacked an intellect that would provide him with an opportunity to offer anything to anyone.

"No ..." the young man replied. "He was writing stories in English – real, unprecedented stories. I stole one with the English title 'Crack'. In Arabic that would be *sad*. Without his knowledge, I sent it to a major African literary competition, and it won first prize."

"Really?"

"Yes, really. Why not? Do you know how much money the prize was? It was 3,000 dollars."

"Really?" I repeated this word unconsciously while at the same time feeling miserable that I hadn't noticed a gifted writer, who was reciting imaginative stories. Perhaps his insanity had diverted me from paying attention to him or perhaps my zeal for and preoccupation with pursuing Nishan had turned off the psychic camera I have long used to snap familiar and unfamiliar shots.

"Really? Where is Murtaja now?"

"I don't know. His family received the prize and left the district secretly, without anyone knowing where they went."

"Pity! I would have liked to meet him."

I said that to humor this youth's excitement, because I knew that neither a prize nor any other delight could improve the life of a person who continued to wander between the ebb and flow of life's tides, as the psychiatrist had remarked when discussing Nishan. It occurred to me at the same time to search for Murtaja's name and the prize he had won. I knew that residents of distant, blighted districts like this – even when they were educated – offered exaggerated descriptions at times and might refer to a scrawny ewe as if it were a raging bull or a narrow alley as if it were the Champs Élysées in Paris or London's Edgware Road. I once heard about a painter who lived in a district like Wadi al-Hikma and who was said to have painted the entire world. I didn't think that was true and went to see his pictures only to find that they were merely ridiculous sketches that didn't rise to the level of being paintings. An aged mechanic who was working on my car in a workshop and who lived in the district of al-Qama'ir, which was also a distant one, claimed that he had prepared the vehicle in which a former president fled on the day of the revolution against him. Of course, that was a fiction or merely a hope, because the flight to which he referred and the accomplices' identity were a matter of public record.

All at once the young man challenged me with a sentence that I hadn't been awaiting or expecting as his eyes gleamed hostilely. "By the way, Sir, I am the person who read your novel *Hunger's Hopes*, which enraged me, and I brought it to Nishan for him to see the crime you had committed against him. I am Shu'ayb Zuhri, a graduate of the college of Public Relations, and have been unemployed for more than four years."

So this was the fellow who had awakened the disaster from its slumbers and cloaked my life with an existence that had never been mine previously. This was the guy who had unleashed a libertine lunatic on me, transforming me overnight into a hunted beast that gradually developed into a pursuer of its prey, after Nishan and I traded places.

Who was pursuing whom in a text as intensely realistic as this?

I actually wasn't a hunter, even though the hunter had fled from me, thus granting me the distinction of becoming a hunter. I was the prey. Pursued by a feeling of torpor because I hadn't yet hit upon a realistic ending suitable for the fictitious text I wrote (or that Nishan wrote — who knew?).

I had recounted my telepathy tale to my brother, Muzaffar, when he returned from his post in the west of the country. The next morning, with extraordinary resolve he announced his suspicions, which alarmed me. He thought the situation was a drama concocted by a poor neighborhood that wished to grow rich at the expense of an author they assumed to be wealthy. According to this scenario, Nishan Hamza was merely a freebooter who claimed to be insane and changed his name and personal information to match the novel's details — not the other way around. His ID could have been counterfeited by an obscure clerk working in the office that issued identity cards or even by an errand boy who fetched tea and coffee there. The faces could easily have been switched; even nationality, which we hold sacred, can be acquired by a fisherman in the Seychelles Islands without much effort.

He asked me, "Do you remember Aunt Jalila, who hosted a television program called 'Benefactor' that went off the air ten years ago?"

"Yes, I remember."

"Do you remember her final show?"

"Yes. I remember when she announced she had discovered that the funds that donors contributed to her program had not been disbursed to any of the needy. She had found out that merchants and high-ranking government officials and even some undersecretaries in government ministries had divvied the money up among themselves, using fake IDs."

"Fine . . . so rid yourself of your fantasy. Restrict your creative imagination to the hours when you are writing. *Hunger's Hopes* is your novel and no one else's."

I wasn't convinced by what he said, especially since Muzaffar had always been quick to suspect people, ever since we were children. I remember that some of his suspicions bore no relationship to reality whatsoever. I was, however, able to convince him that we had to follow the tale to its conclusion, now that we were halfway through it. We would go to Wadi al-Hikma and other similar neighborhoods that might harbor a person like Nishan.

Zuhri was still standing before me, and a number of local residents had begun to encircle us. They may have been motivated merely by curiosity, but even so, I felt tense. I wanted to tell him that I had written my novel from my mind and had never suspected it was a telepathic text or a text that mimicked real life. What had happened would remain an uncanny mystery. If I ever worked out an explanation, I would come in person to tell him.

Zuhri suddenly grew less hostile. He adjusted his straw hat, poked his right hand in the pocket of his shorts, pulled out a folded paper like a page from a student's notebook, and said, "I write stories too. Here's one of my efforts that I like. It's a flash story called 'A Don Quixote with Absolutely No Connection to Cervantes'. I would like to hear what you think of it, please."

"A Don Quixote with Absolutely No Connection to Cervantes" – what an imaginative title! It was beautiful! What a strange district this was where people took an interest in culture and education despite their poverty. I would listen to Zuhri's story. It might be as fine as its title, and perhaps if I praised it profusely I could win him over.

Light green: his shirt.
Gloomy black: his trousers.
What slumbers in his pocket: the spider of poverty.
What gleams atop his head: his bald pate.
What dies in his chest: his heart.
Lacking a profusion of windmills to fight,
He chooses to fight his woman.

Umm . . . a depressing story that truly did not resemble Cervantes; actually there was nothing in it that had anything to do with him. He should have left the title without any story.

Abd al-Qawi the Shadow says that in situations like these he affects the language of dotage and devises a lingo that is all obfuscation to discourage a would-be infiltrator from attempting to follow the path of creativity. But I wouldn't do that, if only out of respect for a boy who had read my damn novel and who would never understand why it was the way it was. I would say his was an excellent story that fully demonstrated his talent. Thus I would soften the stern look on his face and the hostility in his eyes. I would award him a statement that might leave him feeling partial to me.

"Excellent, Shu'ayb Zuhri . . . an extremely beautiful story! You are indeed talented, and I hope to hear more from you on another occasion. Tell me: Do you know where we can find Nishan?"

I think he felt cheered, and he was definitely breathing in a more relaxed way, but he didn't thank me or answer my question about Nishan. Instead, he asked me for my cell phone number, which I felt obliged to give him despite my intense vigilance regarding my phone and home. He recorded my number on his old Ericsson phone, which looked the worse for wear and almost defunct. He strode away rapidly, without demonstrating any desire to help in any manner. Before disappearing completely from sight, though, he pivoted abruptly and returned to us. His face had stiffened. Once he was near me, he said, "Man, you know what upset me most about *Hunger's Hopes*? It was the cover — absolutely the worst cover I have ever seen. Why did they put a picture of a slaughtered chicken on it? The novel's not about a chicken — whether butchered or running free."

Then he turned and departed once more, without awaiting my response.

I had actually had the same reaction. This boy — despite his vulgarity and use of gutter language in addressing me — seemed knowledgeable about book controversies and was the type of reader who begins perusing a book with its cover, exploring in depth the book's presentation and analyzing it acutely. I remember that when this cover design was shown to me before publication, I asked what the point of the cover art was and how it related to the novel. The publishing house's designer, who was almost seventy and whose name was Adam — people called him Father Adam, after the Prophet Adam — retorted rudely,

"Writing a novel is one thing, and designing a cover for it is something else." In short, I shouldn't object to a cover I didn't like, because I lacked the qualifications. The butchered chicken was an appropriate symbol for hunger. If I would just use as much imagination as I did in writing, I would discover the eyes of orphans, widows, and migrants gazing insatiably at this chicken from a distance. I didn't argue with him and left him to his whispered misgivings and artistic hullabaloo. He was the most conceited graphic artist I have ever encountered.

We found Nishan's shack easily this time, even though all the district's structures which I had described sight unseen in the novel, resembled each other. I had created a mental map of the landmarks leading to it, and just in front of me was the corroded metal skeleton of what apparently had once been a truck, which might have been the one Nishan's cousin Zakariya drove before he married an Ethiopian and migrated with her.

The shack was just as I had first seen it: filthy and foul-smelling. Books and ragdolls were scattered across the floor. A kerosene cooker lay haphazardly beside a lantern with a shattered glass shade. Aluminum pots and pans were strewn hither and yon. I noticed a bundle of old papers crammed inside one of the books. I pulled them out and dusted them off, sneezing. The penmanship was poor but legible. Presumably it was Nishan's own handwriting, because he had learned to write at an advanced age. Contrary to my expectations, it wasn't law school homework or any other type of homework. It was a botched attempt at drafting what the opening title proclaimed to be: "A Theory of the Ugliest Sin."

I had never heard of a theory like this and never would have thought that anyone would have created one. A strange curiosity drove me to start reading what I assumed was the genuine raving of an insane man, who had become lost inside my novel's text and was currently lost physically – regardless of whether these two forms of getting lost converged or not.

You talk a lot about this sin. To remain silent about it is uglier than the sin itself.

To love a girl who does not love you is a sin. For you not to love her is even uglier than the original sin.

To be hasty is a sin. For you not to be hasty is even uglier than the original sin.

I stopped reading and returned the papers to their place in the middle of the book. Then Muzaffar and I set off on a taxing tour of the district by foot. We investigated anything that could serve as a hideout – even the houses Hajj al-Bayt had once said were dens of iniquity where hellfire resided. Eventually we reached the abandoned railroad track where we had found Nishan the last time and grabbed him.

Boys were playing ball there and making a racket, and cheery girls were strolling through the ruins, but we found nothing more. A smokestack spewed black smoke in the distance; a secluded factory or refinery must be hiding there.

When we had decided to leave the district and were passing by the carpets used for sales and purchases, we found Zuhri there with his folded piece of paper. He seemed to be reading "A Don Quixote with Absolutely No Connection to Cervantes" out loud to a pair of surly girls, one of whom had her arm slung over the other girl's shoulder.

When eventually, after similar fruitless tours of other districts, we reached my house, my first thought was to turn on my computer to search for Murtaja on Wikipedia and his African prize of 3,000 dollars.

I typed Murtaja's name into the search window on Google, in English in a number of different ways, and then added the word "crack" to this search request, but found no trace of any successful creative activity or prize – major or minor – associated with any Murtaja listed. I found Murtaja Tarbush, an atomic scientist, who was of Middle Eastern heritage, had worked in America for many years, and had died five months earlier of a heart attack. There was Murtaja Mahsud, a Pakistani for whom an international arrest warrant had been issued on charges of terrorism and belonging to al-Qa'ida. He was not to be confused with Murtaja Abd al-Haqq who was a fortune-teller and psychic advisor, Murtaja Isa Kaluk, a notary public in love with the singer Shakira, whom he referred to as an icon of beauty and love, and other Murtajas who were mere names devoid of salient information, swimming in the vast expanses of Google.

I surmised that Zuhri had been exaggerating. Perhaps some short story actually had won something, but not a major competition by any means. I turned off the computer and went to sleep, leaving Muzaffar to chat with a woman on his laptop. Even so, the portrait of Linda shone in living color, as it always did when I pictured her in my mind. Linda the Shadow. I would soon, very soon, sketch her into my life.

13

T HE SHADOW ROSE FROM his relaxed, half-reclining position, removed his slim reading glasses, making his eyes seem slightly smaller than before, and held out a hand that was firm despite the blue veins that spread across its surface.

He didn't seem to notice Muzaffar, or perhaps he had but hadn't shown that he had, because Muzaffar was certainly within his field of vision.

He remarked, "You look extremely elegant, Writer – as if you had come to propose to a girl."

I was slightly perturbed by his sentence and heard Muzaffar say, "As a matter of fact, Mr Abd al-Qawi, he has come for that reason."

The Shadow then noticed my companion, greeted Muzaffar with a bewildered nod of his head, and said to me, "I finished reading *Hunger's Hopes*, luckily for you, and, as you can see, am now reading *Invisible Cities*, this amiable novel by the astonishing Italo Calvino. In my opinion, *Hunger's Hopes* is an excellent novel that could support a sequel, which would begin with the tears of Ranim, who – as you wrote – emigrated and will, I hope, return from her hegira to become Yaqutah once more. She is weeping for her true love and recalling her days with him. This time you will write the novel yourself without telepathy, because your hero has died of cancer. By the way, what has become of him?"

I expected his arrogance. That wasn't a problem, but a sequel for that damn novel was the last thing I needed. Ranim returns from exile and becomes Yaqutah again. Yes, she remained Yaqutah to the final page of the manuscript, but was this really happening? Was it possible that there would be one and the same ending for the real-life story and the fictitious one?

"Yes," I said. "Definitely. Your opinion makes me very happy, and I will try to draft a sequel as soon as my inspirations coalesce. Nishan Hamza fled more than three weeks ago from the psychiatric hospital I checked him into, and unfortunately we haven't found him yet. Even the police have done their best and failed."

"I'm sad to hear that," the Shadow replied. "Father Matthew completed the play *An Elderly Demon in the Republican Palace* down to the last line, but apparently you're not so lucky."

His voice changed suddenly, becoming monstrous and strident. "Why have you actually come to call, Gentlemen?"

I decided not to hesitate to embark on this adventure calmly, despite the less than welcoming sound of his voice and the facial expression which right then was that of a dyspeptic old man.

"Master, with your permission, I have come to ask for your daughter's hand in marriage. This is the reason for our call."

Now the Shadow sat straight up on the edge of his wooden bed. He placed his head in his hands, looking like any father caught off guard by an unexpected suitor for his daughter. I assumed that he was weighing the implications of accepting or rejecting my offer. At that moment I realized the faux pas I had committed. I hadn't factored in my status and age — or my fame, which surpassed that of the Shadow and of all the members of his generation. It struck me that climactic moments occur in real life as well as in writing. I had been engrossed in the conundrum of *Hunger's Hopes* and hadn't liberated myself from it just to plunge into a new riddle. At that instant I wished I could turn back the clock a minute, back to when my mouth was closed and my tongue wasn't spitting out outrageous proposals.

I was beyond the age when it would be seemly to sit smiling next to a woman decked out as a bride together on a pair of velvet chairs for a wedding party or to dance dizzily at the center of a circle of well-wishers. Many details had defeated me, and now I was awaiting a major rout — expulsion from the Shadow's home and friendship.

I turned to reassure myself with the expression of my suspicious brother, Muzaffar, but didn't find him. He had doubtless fled the scene.

The Shadow didn't throw me out. When he stood up and placed his feet in his black slippers, he did not appear to be planning to do that. He replied with a despondency I had never heard in his voice before. "Fine, Writer. You aspire to become part of the family. Let us go inside together and consult the girl to see whether she will accept or not. Please come with me."

I replied in a faint voice, "You go, Master, and I'll wait for you."

"No," he replied decisively.

I trailed after him, feeling a little agitated. We entered the door by which I had seen the girl with slim breasts and short, curly hair exit and enter. Dr Hazaz had also emerged from it.

The Shadow led me with noticeable feebleness down the narrow hallway, which had rooms on either side. The paint was peeling off the white walls and some inexpensive works of art had been hung here and there. One of these was a copy of a painting by the Italian painter Giovanni Boldini and portrayed a young girl embracing a cat with thick fur. Another, which symbolized nature's wrath, was by the Ethiopian painter Simhan Zamzam, who had lived and died without achieving any recognition.

We stopped at the end of the hall, in front of a closed door. The Shadow did not knock. Instead he opened it cautiously and asked me to enter.

I was in a rather small room that was painted rose. Its walls were decorated with many objets d'art made from gold and silver embroidery on pasteboard. The skin of an animal – perhaps a jackal or a fox – hung on the wall opposite us. Several rose-colored wardrobes were placed in the corners, and a broad table covered with books also held what seemed to be a late-model cell phone. The bed in the center of the room was also painted rose.

The lighting was extremely dim, but I saw the girl who was lying on the bed and gasped.

This was by no means the woman I had sketched in my mind. She did not resemble any portrait a lover would try to draw. She was not even suitable for the fantastic imagery of dreams gone awry. Simply put, Linda the Shadow was a tragic girl with misshapen limbs and looked like a ragdoll. She was surrounded by medical apparatus and breathed oxygen from a gauze mask over her face. I remembered how distant her voice sounded; I had described it as a voice rising from a dream or the remnants of a dream. I remembered her intermittent, gasping breaths and understood that this was the halting respiration of a person struggling to stay alive, not the breathiness of a portrait pausing to inspire seduction. Feeling dizzy and weak-eyed, I twisted my face toward the door. I stumbled out, and the Shadow followed me. I heard his voice from very far away: "This is Linda, Renowned Author. She suffers from Becker's Muscular Dystrophy, which is caused by mutations in the genes and affects remote muscles first and gradually progresses to the patient's respiration and stops it. We discovered her condition when she was two years old. She has struggled together with us to learn and to educate herself. She does not have much longer to live now. Do you understand why she hasn't come to talk to you face-to-face, Writer? Do you understand why she hasn't spoken with you by telephone recently?"

Yes, I understood. I could have understood even better if the Shadow had begun to weep in front of me or had allowed me to weep to my heart's content in his house. I looked at him. His face was rigid, and his features seemed chiseled from stone. In his eyes were what I imagined to be the larvae of tears his severity had killed.

14

I CANNOT DESCRIBE THE DRAB days that I spent, feeling more emotionless even than the days when I first couldn't sleep because of the riddle of Nishan and *Hunger's Hopes*. This wasn't because I had lost Linda Abd al-Qawi the Shadow, who would have been − had I been in love with her as a real person − a woman who inevitably would have tidied up my house and my insipid life, filling both with flowers and aromatic plants. I wasn't actually in love with her but with the portrait I had sketched determinedly in my mind and then insisted on seeing in what turned out to be her devastated form.

My feelings were absent without leave because of my compassion for Linda. This was the compassion that bursts forth when we witness an obvious tragedy that is hard to take and that forces us to blame it and curse it as we stand by unable to fight it, to destroy it, or to transform its debris into joy.

I began to wish the tragedy would stop battering the Diligent Reader and allow her at least to pant, to change the pitch of her voice while it sought to create, to allow her half-closed eyes to relish books and her limp hands to grasp a mobile phone and dial a number.

Nishan Hamza no longer interested me: whether he lived or died or wrote a hundred novels comparable to *Hunger's Hopes* and transmitted them via his tedious, silly telepathy. The ending I had endeavored to learn no longer interested me nearly as much as the end, which I didn't want to learn about, of someone like Linda, whom I had out of excessive egoism wanted for my wife . . . when all she aspired to was to continue living.

I was terribly alarmed whenever my phone rang, expecting it would be the stern, arrogant Shadow with the larvae of tears buried alive in his eyes, calling to inform me of his daughter's passing. I would check the number and feel relief that it wasn't the Shadow's or that of any of his acquaintances. At times I would answer the phone and at other times I would rebel against replying. During those futile days I attempted to diminish my isolation a little to keep myself from joining Nishan and becoming a resident in al-Nakhil Private Hospital.

I began to frequent coffeehouses I had previously patronized, with friends or readers who had a claim to my friendship because of all the times I had encountered them in my life. Occasionally I would talk excessively and laugh pointlessly. I knew for certain that I was expending all my feigned delight outside my house, because seclusion would scatter any harbingers of delight that tried to burst forth.

Many people spoke to me by phone. Najma rang me a number of times but I didn't answer her. I went on her Facebook page during a moment of relaxation but was surprised to find that she had unfriended me. Even so I was able to read her page's contents without being able to comment. There was a new picture of her, wearing a red track suit and Adidas shoes. She announced that she would be presenting a new lecture featuring Isa Warif as her guest. He was the cultured, world-class runner who had carried the Olympic torch on one of its stages. "He will discuss the organization of health and sports and grant us hope of living healthily and dying of anything except illness." This time the lecture was being held in the Elegance Health Club in the center of the city. She was on its board of directors.

There were no new posts of her sentiments or atrocious stories, and I didn't find any of the flash essays she customarily put on the page and that earned hundreds of "likes".

The truth was that it didn't matter to me whether she unfriended me or put my picture on her homepage. I don't know why I had entered the page and why I followed the progress of a girl I had categorized as a disaster since we first met. Our meeting in the Juwana Café had reinforced that categorization. She ought to be part of a past that had departed, leaving behind no memories worth recalling.

The girl who manufactured a tragedy and danced to its funereal dirges, who had plotted maternity with a pen on paper, sans emotion, might obtain it and might not, but the only flame she would light in the mind of a novelist would be the silly fire pits he earnestly attempts to keep from igniting in his writing. Many people, as usual, had posted "likes", and many had commented profusely on her fiery red outfit. No one had posted even a terse greeting for the world-class runner who had carried the Olympic torch.

What I term "fictitious deceit" occurs if faces and emotions are different when an author's pen writes in a vast expanse as opposed to a back alley or street. I had known — and the miserable petition writer had too — that this entire online fictitious following meant no more to Najma than a pesky gnat she could easily annihilate whenever she wanted.

I still felt languid, even after reading Najma's page, and with the same languor clicked on my own page, where I posted a poem about death in a number of couplets and attributed it to a fictitious Mexican poet. I called the poem "The Imminent Death of a Reader" and identified the poet as Sebastian Ablino. I didn't wait to see if anyone would "like" it or post a comment and proceeded to the page of "The Virtuous Sister" Nariman, merely to distract myself, nothing more.

Her page was flaming that day, perhaps more than ever before. New names had joined forces to heat it up: Shaved Mustache, Mullah Umar, The Only Man who Loves Veiled Women, A Refugee to Your Eyes, and a woman who called herself "Help!" On every post on the page she wrote: "Help! Help me!"

There was a romantic poem from The Yearning Sheikh, who said it was one of his choicest poems and that he was publishing it for the first time in response to popular demand, even though no one had actually wept or implored him to publish this poem. In short, he was posting it merely because he wanted to.

> Poetry boils in my sad heart,
> Inscribing poems on the brow,
> And beneath the face veil are the ashes of a face,
> But the splendor of the buried secret,
> Even if the feelings are veiled,
> I will certainly read.
> When Nariman appears, we are joyous.
> When she vanishes, you find we feel lost.
> Her presence seems a call to love
> And to dreams that appear clear but are not explicit.
> Were it not for my beard and white hair,
> I would repeat my poems endlessly.

No one had marked this poem with a "like" except The Yearning Sheikh himself. It was followed by what I imagined was a tepid "like" that had slipped from the sarcastic fingers of The Virtuous Sister. Someone named Student of Religious Science had accused the Sheikh of succumbing to temptation and of always being on a suspect page. The Sheikh had responded that Romantic poetry had never been forbidden, provided it was chaste and designed only to display one's talent. Addressing this Student of Religious Science, he asked, "If this is a seductive page, why are you on it?"

I tried to smile but couldn't. I directed my imagination for a number of minutes toward that putative Nariman. I imagined her once as a girl who had a desiccated heart and dangled excessive seduction in the path of innocent individuals whom she carefully chose. Then I changed my mind and imagined Nariman as a wastrel boy composing, for eventual release, a scandalous book in which these evedentiary, incriminating trifles would be featured.

I finally quit the site when my languor disappeared, and the torn picture of Linda the Shadow jumped piece by piece before me.

I had made a huge error when I gave my cell phone number to Shu'ayb Zuhri, the young man from Wadi al-Hikma who wrote the story that was totally unrelated to Cervantes. My phone was busy most of the day with Zuhri's damn messages, which contained flash stories that I was supposed to read and comment on. I didn't have the strength even to peruse a traffic sign while I was driving, but the writer's insistence finally moved me to cast a few quick glances at his stories. I discovered a story called "Whisper", which read: "I whispered to the cloud, and the cloud heard my whisper." Another story, which was named "The Outcast" read: "I found our neighbors' dog in a district dozens of kilometers from ours. I asked her, 'Why are you here, bitch?' She replied, 'It's not because one of your neighbors cast me out of their house, even though they don't have food for breakfast, lunch, or supper.'"

I started to reply to this inanity with a comment even more inane but refrained at the last moment. It wouldn't hurt me to deceive a fantasist and let time teach him wisdom, just as it had taught me. Perhaps he would grow up one day. I wrote him: "Astonishing, Zuhri. You're on the right track."

One morning my doorbell rang while Umm Salama was putting the house in order with her muddled, lame management. That day she was peeved because one of her adolescent sons had seen a new mobile phone – a Samsung Galaxy Note – which would allow him to maintain continuous, secret communication with his guy friends and perhaps even with some girls he knew through free chat apps like Firebird and WhatsApp. He had threatened to leave home and live on the streets sniffing gasoline if she didn't get it for him. I promised to obtain this phone for her two sons, feeling I couldn't believe I had made such a promise when my income, although it came from various sources, wasn't large enough to satisfy the ambitions of adolescent boys who had never realized that they had been born of the womb of a mother who struggled to support them.

I opened the door myself, surprised to find that someone was knocking on my door, on which no one usually ever knocked. I was stunned to see the lad Shu'ayb Zuhri before me, wearing a broad straw hat and a gray necktie inside out. I noticed that the tie's brand name was Shashu, which I had never heard of before. He had a cigarette butt in his mouth and carried a thick brown notebook. The person beside him looked familiar, but I couldn't place him at that precise moment.

How had Zuhri found my house? Who had directed him to the gate of my secluded hideaway, which he had desecrated so simply?

I was thinking this over, and my mind was severely distressed. Zuhri's damn stories had filled my old Nokia phone's memory. I would erase them, and they would immediately be restocked. I hadn't paid much attention to them recently, after I grew used to them. Now, however, I felt upset because from today forward my house stood defenseless.

"How did you find your way here?" I asked Zuhri as I attempted to show that I wasn't suffering from cramps, heartburn, or a surge in blood pressure.

Zuhri was quite composed, as perfect as a disaster. His companion – who was about sixty-five I guessed from the appearance of his face, his still eyes, and his scruffy beard – was searching for something in his pockets, perhaps a cigarette or a pouch of tobacco, I wasn't sure.

Zuhri replied, "Normal, very normal. Since you live in this country, anyone who wants to will be able to find you without any difficulty. You should live at the North Pole or in Australia if you really want to isolate yourself from other people," he added with the worst smile anyone has ever beamed my way. In the process, his cigarette slipped from his mouth and fell to the ground.

I cursed his smile privately with epithets I rarely use in public and at the same time remembered his companion. He was, by God, Asim Ajib, who was known as Asim Revolution, a former Communist. Asim had spent a considerable number of years in the prisons of successive regimes. He wrote impassioned poetry that, in the past, he used to distribute to students in the universities in secret handbills. I had heard recently that he founded or was attempting to found a publishing house, after renouncing

Communism and its gloom. I hadn't seen him for more than twenty years.

"Asim Revolution?" I cried out in disbelief.

The man held out his hand to greet me and, in a voice that tobacco abuse had stripped of all its identifying features, replied, "Asim Ajib. The revolutionary age has ended."

I opened the door all the way and invited them in.

I didn't know what could have linked a former Communist with a poor, obscure short story writer who lived in a construction zone. I could not imagine why they would be visiting me at home, unless the nascent publishing house was the missing link. By God, I didn't want to think that Zuhri's stories would be published. This was another crisis set to hang itself around my neck; I could see myself being asked to write an introduction for the stories. I cursed *Hunger's Hopes* as I always do now when I sink into a new quagmire.

We sat in the library – the living room. It was crammed with books and contained excellent leather armchairs. My visitors' eyes widened as they scanned the books, almost melting them. "All these books?" Zuhri remarked.

"Have you really read all of them?" asked Asim Revolution, who had risen from his chair. He reached out and plucked from its resting place on a shelf *A Tale of Love and Darkness* by the Israeli author Amos Oz. It was massive, and the rest of the books on the shelf, which had been leaning against it, rocked when he pulled it out.

"Amos Oz? I haven't heard of him. Is he Jewish?" he asked.

I didn't answer. It wasn't my problem that he hadn't heard of him. Zuhri stood up and seized a copy of one of the cheap novels that are given to me on one of my trips. I had only read two pages of this book.

The time I spent in the company of the two intruders, Zuhri and Asim Revolution, was foul and fatuous. I didn't offer them so much as a glass of water. They attempted to prolong their stay with periods of silence and interrupted sentences, which they repeated at times, while I tried to abbreviate it with a boorishness I rarely resort to but can turn on in trying times.

What happened was that I stumbled upon the complimentary sentence I had used to honor Zuhri the day he read me "A Don Quixote with Absolutely No Connection to Cervantes" in Wadi al-Hikma, when I went there with my brother, Muzaffar, to search for Nishan, other similar sentences I written, without intending anything in particular in them, in response to his insistent text messages that came to my mobile phone, and some further paragraphs that I really hadn't spoken or written, but which had been composed on my behalf. He had written all these down or penciled them in with extreme care and placed my name beneath all these on the back cover of Shu'ayb Zuhri's story collection. It was called *Worst City–Failed State* and would be released shortly by the Nonaligned Publishing House, which belonged to the former Communist Asim Revolution, who aspired to present gifted new authors.

This was the alliance that had undermined my isolation and plundered my time. How could I have been stupid enough to provide him a possibility that wasn't a reality by opening the door to find these two men? As a matter of fact, this wasn't new; I had often been exposed to comparable situations. I remember once discovering a Romance novel – written by someone called Life Pulse–that had on its cover an encouraging comment attributed to me. I did not know who had composed the blurb and could not find out, because the novel had been self-published and the author was himself a ghost. No one had heard of an author named Life Pulse. In newspapers, I had also frequently come across interviews that I hadn't given. These were assemblages of interviews I had granted previously – rewritten in new ways – or else dialogues someone had conducted with himself and attributed to me.

I mentioned to my visitors being embarrassed by views that I had never agreed to, views that might have been meant merely as compliments, and complained of the exploitation of my name without my knowledge. Zuhri, who was killing me with his sinister smile, rebutted my allegation that I didn't know about his plan, pointing out that at least I did now. He also contended that even if I hadn't known, the book's publication would not harm me at all. These were simply remarks I had actually made to him or written to him in text messages. Asim Revolution flared up zealously in a way that reminded me of his past when he would visit us at the university and debate politics in one of the discussion corners that were a characteristic feature of university life at that time.

His theory, which was peculiar to him alone and wasn't suitable for being popularized as a theory that everyone could follow, was that a youthful writer resembled a recently planted seedling that might grow at a slant or die young if no one watered it. On the other hand, it might sprout leaves, bear fruit, and cast extensive shade if everyone took care to water it.

"You are a long-time gardener who used to repeat, 'A gardener can stake leaning branches and can also uproot the tree.' Perhaps you don't like Mr Zuhri's stories. You will, however, cause others to like them if you say they are stories worth reading. So what do you say now?"

"Nothing," I said as I gasped for breath. "Actually, nothing. I will play the part of the gardener. It won't be my fault if this role isn't successful and the seedling dies, in spite of my care for it."

"Beautiful," Asim said.

"Very beautiful," Zuhri added as his tongue moistened his lips. "This is excellent."

The two men had the final section of their pitch prepared and were about to deliver it. I knew that this was the case and sensed from Asim's restlessness and from the way Zuhri kept rising aimlessly and sitting back down that a final significant and perhaps lethal blow would be added to this session of misfortune.

I decided to sock it to myself in order to alleviate its impact. "You also want me to finance the publication, isn't that so? How much will it cost?"

This thrust seemed to have greatly relieved Asim Revolution, because his narrow eyes, which were exhausted from the weight of a lifetime, smiled and his meager white mustache danced a little jig. Zuhri seemed to be warbling, because I heard something that resembled trills of joy escape from his throat. I was as miserable as could be and attempting to claw my way out of this succession of crises. With extraordinary straightforwardness and without any further internal debate, I agreed to bankroll Zuhri's collection with a sum that was not unreasonable and that was within my means, in addition to contributing the quotes that were attributed to me on the back cover. In this manner I hoped to neutralize one of the crises in order to devote myself to Nishan and poor Linda the Shadow.

No one would blame me for this if he knew my motives, and Zuhri would surely discover a reader who would be dazzled by his disasters and promote them. From my long experience in this field, I knew that even if malaria, rheumatic fever, and whooping cough wrote short stories through some intermediary, they would find readers who would savor their tales and bow respectfully before them. If lesions on the body, pimples, and disgusting secretions were narrated in any language, some reader would exclaim, "By God! By God, splendid!" I will never forget an American novel called *Diabetes*. All that happens in it is that the novelist goes to the bathroom and returns to watch a football game before he passes out. It racked up huge sales one year as readers fell over each other to purchase it.

I wanted these two guests, who were standing up, to leave my house immediately but noticed that Zuhri had left his brown notebook on the table, whether deliberately or inadvertently, I didn't know for sure. I said, "Please don't forget your notebook."

He replied, "I haven't forgotten it. I'm leaving it so you can have a look at the stories as a group. I normally make a copy in another notebook."

They had already departed when the theory, inspired by the cynicism that has haunted Muzaffar, my brother, since he became conscious of the world, leapt suddenly into my mind. Had what happened to my life actually been Shu'ayb Zuhri's devious plot to achieve this precise result – getting me to agree to support his weird literary efforts – meaning that Nishan Hamza had been merely a tool used ingeniously by the educated boy to achieve what he had now?

But such a result did not merit such an ambitious plot. Zuhri could have exerted pressure on me in some other less dangerous manner than this. He could have dispatched a respected friend to me to praise him. Besides, Imam Hajj al-Bayt had declared that Nishan Hamza actually was insane and that they were accustomed to his seasonal attacks. I didn't think a religious man like Hajj al-Bayt would have become a tool in a plan as contemptible as this. Hajj al-Bayt had also referred to the truck driver Zakariya, a relative of Nishan's, as living in Wadi al-Hikma, marrying a girl from Ethiopia, and leaving the country with her. He too had been a character in the novel.

I didn't intend to cast aspersions on Hajj al-Bayt, but they headed his way despite my intentions.

Finally, where had Nishan gone when he fled from al-Nakhil Hospital?

Really – where had he gone?

This was what I had not been able to ascertain. There didn't seem to be any possibility of finding out.

I deferred my suspicions for a time and began, motivated only by boredom and despair, to flip through the brown notebook that contained Shu'ayb Zuhri's collected stories — all of them, or so he said. Filled with the small, deliberate script characteristic of adolescent girls, the notebook was heavy and chockfull.

I read:

Giraffe

They placed her in a little cage in a crowded zoo. When they looked for her a number of days later they found her suckling the little cage with her tits.

As Wakeful as an Ant

A beggar asked me one day: "Can you sleep without giving a beggar alms?"
I replied, "Have no fear. I'm as wakeful as an ant."

Contradiction

Near the Republican Palace I came upon contradictory opinions. I listened to some of them and my destiny changed.

Love

My true love asks, "What need is there for your talk about hearts — so long as you don't pay the dowry and don't marry me?" I replied that she's the one who concludes the marriage.

I quickly lost interest, because I didn't understand the point of these stories, which seemed to be mere arrangements of words, devoid of any pulse or narrative tension that would attract a reader. I started searching for the story "Worst City – Failed State", from which the title of the collection was taken, thinking it might have some deeper significance. I finally found it halfway through the notebook. I was caught off guard when I discovered nothing but the title and a hundred question marks beneath it. These constituted the whole story.

– 15 –

I DON'T KNOW WHEN MY suspicions regarding Nishan Hamza Nishan overpowered me with even greater audacity and completely seized control of me, but it most probably happened a number of days after the demise of Linda the Shadow. Her muscular dystrophy overwhelmed her respiration and had finally arrested it.

This was no easy blow to bear. It had been days and perhaps months since my portrait had been torn to pieces. I was reassembling its parts in my mind and restoring their beauty, whenever I had time alone.

Abd al-Qawi the Shadow delivered the news himself, one afternoon when I was drowning in the seas of my everyday life. After ending my self-imposed isolation, I was sitting by myself in a coffeehouse waiting for a literary critic I had promised to meet. I was thinking about everything and nothing in particular when I was surprised by a telephone call; despite my forebodings, I took the call.

He said, "Come help us bury your favorite reader, Writer. Linda has died."

Then he hung up.

His voice was choked this time, the voice of a truly old man who was repulsed by the words on his lips. I imagined that it had required enormous effort just to speak in that choking voice instead of being strangled by the ropes of expressions that fathers typically use when they lose their sons or daughters.

I was unable to drive my car or even approach it. I left it where it was parked and took a taxi that pulled up suddenly beside me without my hailing it. I was surprised to find that the driver, who was more or less a young man and wore local garb and whose lower lip bulged with a wad of tobacco, knew me. He had stopped because he recognized me, at a time when cab drivers had become arrogant and wouldn't stop for anyone.

This driver didn't know me as a writer but as a former math teacher who had taught him in middle school. He had not forgotten that I had mistreated him more than anyone else in his life. I had punished him nonstop for extreme inattention and incomprehension of lessons. Because of me, he had been forced to drop out of school and to work at a great number of humiliating jobs, until he ended up as a cabbie. He related to me all my errors: giving him detention in the classroom for many hours while his classmates whispered together, pulling him by his ear in front of the other pupils, calling him a shoeshine boy hundreds of times. My mind caught some of this but not all while a rude song blasted from the vehicle's player: "He fed me noodles when I didn't have a penny and said to me: 'Sleep, dear.'" I was forced to apologize to him in a feeble voice — totally unlike the harsh voices of teachers — for my severity, which

I had thought was in his best interest. I honestly didn't remember all the forms of punishment that he rattled off and don't think they would have come naturally to me even when I was a teacher. The taxi driver accepted my apology good-naturedly and deposited me in front of the cemetery. The driver refused point blank to accept his fare, repeating, "By God Almighty, your fare is dedicated to the deceased woman. We are God's and to Him we return."

We buried the distinguished reader in al-Salatin Cemetery, an old cemetery on a neglected road on the outskirts of the city. It enjoys a prestigious reputation, and its history dates back to the era of the former kingdoms. It is said that the daughter of the last sultan of the Kingdom of Funj was buried there, but it certainly didn't give that impression. There was nothing except pebbles, dry dirt, and some straggly shrubs, which revived during the rainy season and looked dead during a drought. The Shadow had chosen this cemetery himself, despite his suffering. I knew that he loved it and had spent a number of months living in a shack near it, entering it several times a day to help people bury their dead so he could write a play that focused on the dead. The play, "The Sultan's Hand," was performed in the late 1970s. I attended it when I was still a teenager and not at all tuned in to art and writing.

The loss was obviously great, and the funeral was crowded with many people I knew and many I didn't. I saw Sonia al-Zuwayni, the Moroccan proprietor of hair salons, swathed in mourning black; I wouldn't have suspected that she knew the Shadow well enough to share in the family's sorrow in this manner. I also observed Professor Hazaz, the reflexologist, as nimble as ever, but his face looked a little different. The glamorous star Mustafa Khalifa was there, along with a number of poets, novelists, and dramatists, as well as the retired female vocalist Zakiya the Nightingale. The Shadow told me once, when he was in a good mood, that they had loved each other madly. A young writer with bushy hair, who had published a novel called *Futile Yearning* two years earlier, approached me and told me in a whisper that the deceased woman had spoken to him by telephone and discussed his talent and his novel enthusiastically, asking him to write more novels because he had a distinctive style. He admitted that when he heard her tremulous, breathy, languid, inspirational voice he had never imagined she was a girl who was fighting to survive.

So I wasn't the only person whose writing Linda had fallen in love with and I wasn't the only man who had sketched a dazzling portrait of The Reader. Perhaps he was also recalling her on drab nights. I happened to be the one who had seen his portrait ripped to shreds.

When I was most deeply immersed in the prevailing atmosphere of tragic loss, I spotted Najma. I tried to avert my face from her eyes as best I could but failed. It was the same new Najma who had updated herself as part of a plan to achieve motherhood without bothering with the preliminaries; she had not reverted to her former classic self. She was walking in Linda's funeral procession, after decking herself out, applying cosmetics, and allowing her hair, which she had dyed blonde this time, to extend enticingly beyond her light headscarf. She actually looked more like a girl in a bridal procession than someone at a funeral.

I suddenly found Najma beside me, very close to me, and almost touching me – in spite of the oppressive burden of the tragedy – while men's eyes, which could brush aside every other distraction, collided with her and me. I felt agitated. She asked, "Why are you ignoring me, Master? Why haven't you returned my calls?"

I didn't know how to respond. I had made a firm decision not to reply to her calls. My feelings had instituted that policy and my humane tendency, which no doubt is shared by most other people, had confirmed it. I almost blurted out, "Why would I answer a girl who is a calamity?" All the same, I was afraid she might collapse or become hysterical in this mournful place and at a time when an outburst would be totally inappropriate. I knew from personal experience that personalities like hers were capable of creating any type of spectacle for no reason at all. So I said, "I haven't found the time. I've been absurdly busy."

She replied, after, I imagined, carefully filling her sentence with traps before she uttered it. "I was contacting you to tell you what I thought of three of your novels that I have recently read. You're a brilliant writer, and your friendship makes me very happy as does your advice, which will help my writing in the future."

She didn't mention the name of the three novels she had read. I swear she hadn't read more than half a page out of my thousands of pages of works. Had we not been at a funeral, I would have asked her about the books and inundated her with questions about characters and events and what she derived from reading the novels. Of course I wouldn't do that, and she knew this perfectly well, because she could see my misery and that of the real people with whom she was saying farewell to Linda the Shadow.

They had begun the funeral rituals when Najma left me, after pressuring me to meet her soon. Now I was able to breathe, to weep silently, and to extend my hand to help lower Linda into the great beyond and to try to support the Shadow to keep him from falling, despite his heroic composure, which I sensed was very fragile and could shatter at any moment. I was listening without much interest to a sermon delivered deliberately and expertly by a man of sterling faith, when I noticed Luqman the Shadow, or Loco with a Shadow, run up from the distance. He was short and plump, and his hair was in cornrows. He wore yellow, reflective glasses, jeans that were ripped at the knees, and a T-shirt adorned with a color portrait of the late singer Michael Jackson.

Evening had fallen when Loco arrived. Notwithstanding his long period of exile and his appearance, which didn't fit our society, he retained his sense of solidity with our community and had come when he learned that his sister had died.

I HAVE MENTIONED THAT MY suspicions began to get the better of me, especially when Nishan Hamza disappeared from my life and from the city's hustle and bustle, apparently once and for all.

I began brooding seriously on some aspects of his story that didn't seem to add up. These were matters I had overlooked because of my extreme agitation following Nishan's surprising and upsetting appearance at the Social Harmony Club and his subsequent recital of my novel or most of my novel at the home of Malikat al-Dar, my spiritual mother. My bewilderment had continued for a number of months as this puzzle staggered on without any resolution.

I realized that the soldier Asil Muqado, who had tried to overthrow the government and, in the novel, had been executed but in real life, according to Nishan, had fled to Chad, would be known to the public in this country. Since my birth I had experienced all its periods of upheaval and its peaceful and troubled times, yet I had never before heard of a rebellion spearheaded by a soldier called Asil Muqado.

I delved deeper into my memory and reviewed all the military rebellions that had clawed on the walls of previous regimes or had actually torn them down, from the nation's independence to the present day. I uncovered Colonel Musa Gad al-Karim's rebellion, which only lasted two days before collapsing; Lieutenant General Fadl Allah Zayn al-Kamal's rebellion, which lasted for a number of months but ended bloodily; Samih, the teenager who occupied the broadcasting building one day to win a bet with his girl-friend; Sergeant Kaka Kuku, who came from Jebel Nuba in the west and advocated separation of the Nubians from the Arabs; and even Sabata al-Hazli's rebellion, which was conducted with wooden weapons by a lunatic from al-Qama'ir District as he guffawed. But I didn't come across a rebellion led by Asil in any corner of my memory.

I telephoned some journalists and political analysts skilled in investigating the country's conditions and in blowing them out of all proportion if necessary. They confirmed to me emphatically that our national history lacked any insur-rection of this stripe carried out by a soldier of Chadian heritage – unless the rebels had been very close to the authorities, who then might have hushed up the unpleas-antness to safeguard their own reputation.

So the point remained a bit murky, and I resolved to try to shed light on it if I could find anyone to assist me.

At this time I also discovered that I had concentrated so exclusively on Nishan during those days that I had neglected to verify the existence of a real nurse named Yaqutah who had worked in the psychiatric hospital and then had migrated to newly liberated Libya under a different name. I would not need to investigate her rela-tionship to a former patient named Nishan Hamza, because the mere existence of a nurse by this name – even if she wasn't still working at the hospital – would give the damn text some legitimacy as being true-to-life.

I entered the government psychiatric hospital with a physician I knew who had offered to assist me. The shabby old building, which dated back to the colonial era, continued to serve the same purpose of embracing indigent mental patients, even if its embrace now was foul and frigid and devoid of any emotional warmth. Once inside I discovered, to my astonishment, someone I knew, a man I would never have dreamed would end up with chains shackled to his ankles, especially not in such a place. He was stumbling around the courtyard with difficulty in the midst of dozens of befuddled people. Tough guards were scattered among the nurses, and security officers in blue uniforms were also stationed there. I shouted incredulously, "Ifranji! Joseph!"

The Southerner turned toward me. Here was the man who had been a vagrant in the Aisha Market and the jinni Daldona's lover, the man I had hired as Nishan's caretaker, but who had never performed that duty. His eyes were red and his lips were swollen with exanthema. His hands seemed to have been part of some argument, because they were bandaged in rags.

"Ifranji!"

He did not seem to know me, even though he had caught his name when I lobbed it toward him. His face remained expressionless, and he showed no reaction. Clearly Joseph Ifranji was in some predicament over and beyond being held in a detention center for undocumented aliens, where he had been interned as the authorities prepared to expel him to his new homeland of South Sudan. He had most likely assaulted someone in that camp or had perhaps pretended to be schizophrenic in order to remain in the country longer, while he thought up some new ploy to leave the detention center and resume his life as a vagrant in the Aisha Market. I had forgotten Ifranji — or my affairs had distracted me from him — and I hadn't attempted to secure his release from the internment camp. Now I was confronted by a genuinely insane person or an actor who was capable of realistically portraying insanity.

I rushed toward Joseph Ifranji but found I couldn't move. I almost fell, forgetting that my feet were also shackled with rude iron chains.

A NOTE ON THE AUTHOR

AMIR TAG ELSIR, who was born in the north of Sudan in 1960, currently lives in Doha, Qatar. He has published two biographies, a poetry collection, and fifteen novels. He studied medicine in Egypt and Great Britain and worked for many years in Sudan as a gynecologist before moving his practice to Qatar. He began by writing poetry but shifted to novels in 1987. Among his novels are *Ebola '76*, *The Yelling Dowry*, *The Copt's Worries*, *French Perfume*, and *Crawling Ants*. His novel *Sa'id al-Yaraqat* was shortlisted for the International Prize for Arabic Fiction in 2010 and published by Pearson in the African Writers Series as *The Grub Hunter* in 2012. His novel *366* was longlisted for the International Prize for Arabic Fiction in 2014, and he works as a mentor for creative writing students. English translations of his novels *French Perfume* (Antibookclub) and *Ebola '76* (Darf Publishing) are scheduled for release in 2015. Tag Elsir is the nephew of the beloved and distinguished Sudanese author Tayeb Salih.

A NOTE ON THE TRANSLATOR

WILLIAM MAYNARD HUTCHINS is an American translator of contemporary Arabic literature. Hutchins's best-known translation is *The Cairo Trilogy* by Egyptian Nobel Prize-winner Naguib Mahfouz. He has also translated Tawfiq al-Hakim, Ibrahim 'Abd al-Qadir al-Mazini, al-Jahiz, Muhammad Khudayyir, Ibrahim al-Koni, Fadhil Al-Azzawi, Hassan Nasr, and Mahmoud Saeed. Hutchins has received two US National Endowment for the Arts grants in literary translation. His translations have appeared in *Banipal* magazine and online at wordswithoutborders.org and brooklynrail.org.